The Church at the Fork in the God intended his people to live ~~ j~y ~~~ ~~~~~ weaving into a fictional story the truth of the prayer of Jesus for us to be one. As you read this story, you will find it is not about building a church building, but about building the body of Christ. This story reminds us that you cannot judge based on the outside, but what is in the hearts of each person.

Through a simple yet powerful story, Jay confirms the time-honored principle that actions speak louder than words. I can highly recommend the author as a man of God and commend Jay on the message of oneness in the Lord.

— **Barry Clanton, senior pastor, ChristWay Christian Church, Martinez, Georgia**

In his latest book, *The Church at the Fork in the Road*, Jasper Barber captures the central coastal region of North Carolina—and its people—with words, warmth, and knowledge available only to one who grew up in that special place at that special time. As one who shared that time and place, I congratulate Jay Barber on another fine piece of writing.

— **Gene Price, journalist and retired editor of the *Goldsboro (NC) News-Argus*, and author of *Folks Around Here***

[*The Church at the Fork in the Road* is] a wonderful story of love and redemption, heard most clearly by God's children but spoken to everyone with the heart to see miracles and the courage to accept their part in making them happen.

The author has crafted a heartwarming story that provided this old vet a beautiful reminder that only God can align all our planets!

— **R. Nicholas Carter, Major (Ret), USAF**

Dear reader, you are in for a treat. I first met Jay Barber when I was a young, new teacher, and he had just retired from the military. At the time, I thought he was getting old, but now I am old enough to know that he was still quite young and taking college courses to open doors for his next steps. One of his next steps was to begin writing. His first book, *Memories of the Islands*, was a joy to read. In fact, after reading it, I spent a day driving to the remote river islands that had inspired the story in order to experience that landscape for myself.

In this, his second book, Jay touched the depths of my heart like a harpist plucking strings to create perfect harmonies. His main character, Jack Porter, fulfills forgotten dreams by facing his family roots and fears head on. In doing so, Jack shows us a wonderful path to racial reconciliation in the rural south. That in itself makes the book worthwhile, but more important is the clear message that God has a plan for every life. God is always working in every place, though few people ever receive fame or recognition for the things God chooses to do through them. This is a heartwarming story that will increase your faith in God and in his ability to use humanity in spite of our weaknesses.

— Matt Garrett, retired president of Central Carolina Community College in Sanford, NC

Jay Barber has crafted a story that reflects the soul of a Christian who wants to prove to himself that he is a changed man. Set free from the prejudices of his youth, Jack Porter returns to his roots determined to take that other fork in the road. In reaching out to help his black brothers rebuild the oldest church in the county, he discovers that he has robbed himself of many blessings because of his misguided way of seeing the world. This story shows the power of Christian brothers and sisters working together, not just to rebuild a church, but to build character, relationships, and a better community.

— **Jimmie Ford, retired educator and former county commissioner, Wayne County, NC**

THE CHURCH
AT THE FORK
IN THE ROAD

JASPER E. BARBER

Book Title: The Church at the Fork in the Road
Copyright © 2017 by Jasper E. Barber

TB

Published by Trusted Books
an Imprint of Deep River Books
Sisters, Oregon
www.deepriverbooks.com

ISBN – 13: 9781632694348

Library of Congress: 2017940392

Cover and Interior Illustrations by Rocky Melvin

Printed in the USA

Cover design by Joe Bailen, Contajus Designs

This book is dedicated to my wife, Mary Jane Rogers Barber, whose love for her family and friends is constant and unconditional. *It is better to give than to receive* is her motto, and she has given far more than she will ever receive. She would not have it any other way. She is my special angel, the answer to one of my prayers.

TABLE OF CONTENTS

ACKNOWLEDGMENTS

When I look at where I am today and compare it to where I began, I am amazed at how far I have come. Somebody was and still is watching over me, lighting the way, and connecting me with people along life's highway who have encouraged, inspired, and helped to mold me into the person I have become. To all of these I am grateful, and to those in the beginning who must have looked at me with much suspicion, thanks for not giving up on me.

In every community there are those who shine like diamonds among the rocks. One of these in Wayne County is Ms. Elizabeth Meador, currently an adjunct instructor at Wayne Community College. She also writes a weekly column for the Goldsboro *News-Argus* extolling the virtues of the English language. She has dedicated her life to teaching the English language, and no doubt those who have done well under her tutelage have succeeded in their chosen profession.

I was blessed to have her suffer through the first edit, and she did an awesome job. She did this over the Christmas and New Year holidays, and insisted on taking only a pittance for her invaluable work. I can't find the words to adequately express my appreciation. Perhaps I should just say that I am honored to be living in the same county with such a distinguished lady.

A special thanks to Gene Price, one of North Carolina's most respected newspaper editors and writers and author of *Folks Around Here*, and his wife Gloria for their input and encouragement.

Rocky Melvin, artist and fabricator from Goldsboro, North Carolina, worked patiently with me to create the artwork.

A big thanks also to my son Dean for his insight and suggestions.

I cannot thank the folks at Deep River Books enough for their assistance. I'm especially indebted to Ms. Rebekah Tysoe, one of those special people I have met along life's highway, who did the comprehensive edit. Her recommendations were superb, and she took the time to explain why I needed to make many of the changes. Should I write another novel, I will use the new knowledge I have acquired from her.

INTRODUCTION

Whose book this is I think I know
His abode is in the heavens though

I have slightly revised the words to the poem "Stopping by Woods on a Snowy Evening" by Robert Frost, one of America's great poets. These words came to me as I tried to think of what I wanted to say to introduce this first work of fiction that bears my name.

While I am the instrument through which this book has come into being, I certainly do not believe that I can take full credit for its production. Only those who believe that God inspires people to do certain things can fully understand why I say this.

After writing *Memories of the Islands: The Life, Place, and Times of the Barber Family*, I vowed not to write another book unless it offered the reader something more than just a few hours of pleasure. While I believe I have accomplished this, the reader is the final judge.

Although the characters are fictitious, what they have to say is not necessarily so. What has amazed me more than the knowledge that God led me to do this is the fact that the characters are so real to me. If I were an artist, I could draw a real-life image of each character, right down to the dimples in Melanie Epstein's beautiful brown cheeks.

It is my prayer that you will find *The Church at the Fork in the Road* worthy of your time and resources. After you have read it, I hope you can say: "It made me think about my relationship with God and with my fellow brothers and sisters."

PROLOGUE

Thomas Wolfe said you can't go home again, but after forty years in the Air Force Jack Porter was going to do just that.

He knew it would not be the same place he left as a boy to see what the rest of the world had to offer. Now, he had seen enough of the world, from Tokyo to London, and more places in between than he could remember. If there was a better place to settle down and retire, he had not found it, and he was tired of looking.

Jack's parents were deceased, but while they were still living they divided their property among the children in the family. Jack was willed the home and a tract of land at the north end of the huge Porter farm. Only a few acres were tillable; the rest was swamps and ridges. His parents knew this was the land that Jack loved best. Over the past three years he had used his vacations, holidays, and weekends to remodel the old farmhouse, so he was moving to a familiar and comfortable place mostly filled with good memories.

Cobbwebb was not a great name for a county. But Jack loved the motto: Bountiful and Beautiful Beyond Belief, because it described the way he felt about the county.

Formed from two other counties in 1774, it was named for an Englishman named John Cobb and a Native American named Joseph Webb.

The Cobb family came to America around 1700 and moved from Jamestown a few years later to the small village of Winston, a new settlement some fifty miles inland from the Atlantic Ocean on the Poopah River. The Poopah River got its name from the Polongo people who lived further upriver. *Poopah* means muddy waters.

After John Cobb and his wife, Sarah, died, their son Mick took over the family business, a general merchandise store. The Cobb family had been instrumental in organizing and starting the first church and school in the area. Mick's sister, Lizzy, was its first teacher. The A-framed building served as the village church, school, and meeting place for local leaders.

Joseph Webb was an anomaly. From a distance, he looked like the rest of the villagers. The only difference between him and the others was his brown skin, his long ponytail, and his broken English. He and his wife, Monia, lived in a log cabin near the river. He survived by hunting and fishing and by tending a small garden. He did odd jobs for people in the community and was well known and respected. He and Monia were converts to Christianity. Nothing more is known about them, although legend has it that they came from Georgia where a missionary had converted Joseph's parents to Christianity.

They were the only Native Americans living in Winston, the first European settlement in Cobbwebb County. Joseph and Monia were accepted as part of the community, an unusual adjustment for that time.

Conflict with Indians in the area was unheard of. In fact, it was rare that any Indians ever came to Winston, although occasionally some were seen in their canoes going up or down the river.

One afternoon three Native Americans banked their canoe on the Winston side of the Poopah and walked into the village. Joseph was called upon to communicate with them since they didn't speak English. Joseph didn't speak their language either, but he was able to find out they lived upriver and had stopped for food and water.

As the sun began to set, Mick Cobb and his wife, Elle, discovered their ten-year-old daughter Emily was missing. They searched the entire village to no avail. The last time she had been seen was around midafternoon near the river.

Everyone suspected the worst—that she had fallen into the river and drowned or had been taken captive by the afternoon visitors. Joseph Webb had had an uneasy feeling about the visitors. While the rest of the village continued their search for Emily, Joseph grabbed his musket and headed to the river where his canoe was tied to a cypress tree.

He panned the river, wondering which way the Indians would go if they had captured the girl. Joseph decided that downriver would have been too risky as more settlers were there than upriver. So he headed upriver as the sun disappeared below the horizon.

They had at least a two-hour start on him, so Joseph had to move quickly. He was thankful the river was not flooding. because there was less chance of running into debris and paddling was less difficult. He hugged the riverbank to avoid the stronger current in the middle. After four hours he was exhausted and began to wonder if he had gone in the wrong direction. Something within urged him to keep paddling.

Soon he began to hear voices. Hope that not too far ahead Joseph would find what he was seeking revived him. The half-moon and clear skies gave him sufficient light to see by, and he paddled even faster than before. The sound of voices grew louder and louder until he could see a canoe. Something told him it belonged to the three Indians. He banked his canoe where it would not be detected, got out, and stretched his weary legs and body.

After midnight the voices ceased. Joseph slowly and quietly made his way along the riverbank to where the canoers camped. He inspected the camp from a distance as he crept ever closer, searching for Emily. *What if she's not there*, he thought. *What will they do if they find me sneaking up on them in the middle of the night?*

But Joseph was sure he would find Emily with them. He was now close enough to hear them snoring. An owl shattered the silence with its "whoo who, whoo who" cry. Joseph was thankful it did not disturb the campers. He could now see everyone in the camp. There were four bodies with blankets covering them, but he could not make out their faces.

What do I do now? Joseph asked himself. He did not want to kill or hurt anyone, and he certainly did not want any harm to come to Emily, were she among them.

Joseph went to their canoe and paddled it to the other side of the river. There he filled it with dry limbs from downed trees, dead reeds, and dry leaves. He returned to the other side and pulled the canoe up on the bank, half of it still in the river. He set fire to the debris and quickly positioned himself directly behind their camp. He waited as the fire grew from a small flame into a blaze. As the flames grew larger they lit up the area and the snapping and popping of the fire could easily be heard.

Suddenly, one of the Indians awoke and began yelling at the others. The other two awoke and saw that their canoe was burning. They threw off their blankets and ran to help put out the fire. Emily was under the other blanket, tied up. Joseph rushed in and picked her up, covering her mouth with the blanket she slept in, and disappeared into the night. Before placing Emily into his canoe, Joseph uncovered her face so she could see him. She burst into tears of relief. After he untied her hands and legs, she gave him a big hug. As they began the journey home, Joseph could hear her captors yelling and splashing in the river.

Joseph paddled through the night, but going downriver was much easier. He and his happy passenger returned to Winston just as the sun was ushering in a new day. The Cobb family had been up all night. When Joseph returned Emily to Mick and Elle, he thought of a sermon he had heard which spoke of sorrow reigning for the night, but joy coming in the morning.

It was shortly after this adventure that the citizens were given the opportunity to name their county. They wanted to name it Cobb County, but Mick Cobb refused to let them use his name unless Webb was placed beside it.

Though Cobbwebb County is too far from major cities or highways to make it attractive for manufacturing plants or centers of banking, its fertile lands are well suited for producing a variety of agricultural products.

Somehow Jack did not see his return to Cobbwebb County as going home again; he was returning to the place his heart had never left.

CHAPTER 1

SUMMER BROWN

"I can't believe you're returning to Cobbwebb County," Adam Clark said when Jack Porter told him where he planned to settle down after retiring.

"I know," said Jack, "but if we all lived in the same place some of us would die from a lack of oxygen. By going back to this remote part of the state I'm doing folks a favor that live in the big cities."

"Funny. Real funny, Jack. Is Summer Brown going with you?"

"No. I regret that things have not worked out between us the way I had hoped."

"Sorry to hear that. That's all the more reason to stay here. It's going to be mighty lonely in Cobbwebb County all by yourself."

"A man with a great imagination and lots of good memories is never alone, Boss."

"Yeah, but the world has changed since you left there, Jack, and so have you. But I doubt if anything has changed very much in that part of the state. You'll spend all your time butting heads with people who are content with the way things have been and still are. You'll be as outdated in that environment as the Model T."

"I will not argue with you on those points, but someone needs to go to places like Cobbwebb County and try to convince people the world has changed. I may not change anyone, but I want my family and the people I grew up with to know that I have changed, and for the better."

Jack Porter was saying farewell to the best boss he'd had in his forty years with the United States Air Force. He knew his advice was sound and given in his best interest.

Jack thanked Adam for his advice, but he was not going back to be a part of what has always been and still is. He was going back with a new perspective of the world and the people in it. He had been transformed since he left home as a teenager. He had to prove to himself that his transformation had found a home deep within his soul, and there was no better testing ground than Cobbwebb County.

There was another reason Jack was returning to the place where his life began. He felt empty. Gold City, the town near the air base where he had lived so happily with his wife, Misty, and friends for more than twenty years, had suddenly become a place of deep sorrow. Returning to his roots would fulfill a dream, and he could start over. He believed he could find fulfillment there, a new purpose in life. His hometown was a place where he could rise again from the emotional trauma he had experienced and do something he failed to do growing up there.

Misty, who had been a devoted wife, mother, and grandmother, died after suffering from multiple ailments. And two short months later, dear friends of theirs were suddenly separated by death as well. Summer lost her husband Jerry.

While consoling each other over the loss of their spouses, Jack's feelings for Summer moved well beyond friendship. He was falling in love with her. And though she had never come right out and said so, Jack believed that she loved him as well.

Six months after Jerry died, Jack decided to take Summer to The Country Garden Inn, one of the finest restaurants in the immediate area. It was located in the country. Surrounded by pines and oak trees, it was an expensive but tranquil place to enjoy a meal with someone you loved.

Jack had told Summer he was taking her to a special place for dinner but failed to tell her it was located forty miles from Gold City. About half way there, Summer asked Jack if he was lost.

"No. When we get there you will be surprised to find a place like this in the boonies."

"Why haven't you taken me to this place before?"

"Good question. You'll find out over dinner."

They arrived at the restaurant at 5:40 and the parking lot was almost full.

Summer could hardly believe her eyes. The restaurant was huge. Nothing surrounded it but farms. The rustic-style Southern structure fit in perfectly with the pines and oaks that surrounded it and the parking spaces.

"It's gorgeous!" she said. "Why haven't I ever heard of this place?"

"Probably because I'm the only one who loves you enough to bring you here," replied Jack with a smile.

As they walked into the restaurant Summer asked, "Are we going to have to wait to be seated?"

Jack looked at her with a grin on his face. "You don't think I would bring you this far from home to sit for an hour with strangers, do you?"

The waitress met them in the foyer, and when Jack gave her his name they were escorted to their private "Love Bird" room. From there, they could view the garden area where weddings and other special events were commonly held. On this night it was not in use, but still offered a beautiful area to admire while having dinner. Birdbaths and feeders were placed among the trees.

After letting Summer take in the view and the atmosphere and commenting on the name of their room, they looked at the menu. "These prices are out of sight," said Summer. "You could've taken me to a less expensive place, and I would've been just as happy."

"I could have, but I didn't. I sold an acre of prime farm land so I'd have enough money to bring you here," Jack teased. "So quit looking at the prices and find something you want for dinner."

They decided on the beef tenderloin and each chose different vegetables to go with it, along with a salad and fresh country bread, and for a beverage they had sweet iced tea. For dessert they enjoyed a French-style chocolate pie with coffee.

During dinner, Jack and Summer laughed and teased each other about some of the things which had happened to them in the years they had known each other—silly things like the gag gifts they had given to each other for Christmas and birthdays.

Soon after they finished their meal, Jack became more somber. He looked Summer in the eyes and said, "I didn't bring you here tonight just to eat a meal. I brought you here because I want to ask you an important question and I could not let myself do that in a crowded cafeteria or a fast food restaurant."

He paused.

"I never thought I would find another woman I could love as much as I loved Misty. I credit her for turning me into a human being. I thank God for her. But Summer, I also thank God for you.

"I will never forget your comforting presence during Misty's last days and especially to me during the weeks that followed. You were the angel unaware that Misty and I needed. And since then, the times we have been together have brought me nothing but joy."

Jack reached across the table, took Summer's hands, and added, "Summer, you'd make me the happiest man in the world if you'd give me your hand in marriage."

Summer sat for some time, thinking of what she would say. She looked at Jack, withdrew her hands and put them over her face, and bowed her head. She took a couple of minutes to gather her thoughts.

Jack bowed his head too, and asked God to give him the courage to accept her answer, believing that God would work all things for their good.

They looked up at each other. "I have been dreading this because I knew you were going to ask me this question sooner or later. I can't give you an answer, Jack, not because I don't love you and enjoy your company immensely, but because I don't know at this time if I even want to get married again. Maybe next month, or six months or a year from now, I will know what I want, but right now I cannot answer your question."

Jack looked out the window, trying to hide the disappointment that invaded his mind and soul.

"Thank you for being honest with me, Summer. I knew you would be, and your honesty is just one of the many reasons I love you so much. I will honor your request and give you more time."

The return trip to Summer's home was a sad one for Jack. Summer was quiet as well. She invited Jack to have coffee with her but he declined.

"I'm sorry, Jack, that I couldn't give you the answer I know you wanted to hear. Thank you for your patience."

Jack gave her a hug and a kiss and said goodnight.

He was depressed for the next week, although he did a good job of hiding it from Summer and his coworkers.

During the following six months, Jack did everything he could think of to woo Summer into marrying him. He took her to concerts, plays, movies, and to dinner whenever and wherever she wanted to dine. He cut her grass every week, trimmed the hedges and rose bushes, fixed leaking faucets, and repaired the roof when the wind blew off some of the shingles. He even helped her paint two of the rooms in her home. Every week he brought her a small gift or flowers. They went to church together every Sunday. Summer was the happiest person he knew and he enjoyed every minute he spent with her.

The month before he was scheduled to retire Jack discovered that Summer was seeing other men. He tried not to let it bother him because they had not made an agreement to only date each other. Still, Jack had to know if Summer was serious about ever marrying him.

He set up another dinner date, six months to the day after he first asked her to marry him, to find out. He took her to the same restaurant and booked the same room.

On this night, Summer was as happy as he had ever seen her.

"This must be another special occasion," she said.

"It is and I will get into that after we enjoy another sumptuous meal."

As they finished up a delicious dessert, Summer said, "So what's the special occasion tonight, Jack?"

"Remember the last time we dined here, Summer?"

"Yep, I sure do. You asked me to marry you."

"You asked me to give you more time, and I have done that. Over the past six months I have done everything I possibly could to demonstrate my love for you.

"My question tonight is: have I persuaded you to give me an answer?"

"Jack, I'm living a life that I have dreamed about since I was a senior in high school. I am happier than I have ever been. I'm sorry, but my answer is still the same. I need more time."

Jack smiled. "I'm glad that you're happy and living your dream. And I will give you all the time you need. I have an announcement to make tonight, and I pray it will not sever our relationship. I have a dream too, and I was willing to give up my dream if you would marry me. But since you have put me on hold indefinitely, I am going to fulfill my dream."

Alarmed at this revelation, Summer asked, "What are you talking about, Jack? You've never said anything to me about your dream."

"That's true. The reason I have not said anything is because, until now, I have been a part of your dream."

"What's your dream?"

"I am leaving Gold City and returning to the home I grew up in."

"I can't believe you are doing this to me," said Summer in a raised voice. "You are not trying to force me into marrying you, are you? If you are it won't work."

"No. Forced marriages never work. And if you changed your mind right now I would withdraw my proposal. Marriage is sacred to me, and the woman I marry must love me as much as I love her and be totally committed to a lasting partnership."

There was fear in Summer's face and in her voice as she pleaded, "Don't leave me, Jack!"

"I'm not leaving you, Summer. I am moving 80 miles north, a two-hour drive from Gold City. I will come to see you every week, and you can visit me anytime you wish."

"I need you, Jack. Can't you wait just a little longer?"

"I'll be waiting for you, Summer, for as long as it takes, but not in Gold City. I'll still be waiting for your answer in Winston."

"What has caused you to make this sudden decision, may I ask?"

"Over the past six months I have given you everything I have to offer. And apparently I am still missing something that you want. I say this because I have seen you with other men on two occasions."

"You've been spying on me, haven't you?" she snapped.

"No. It never crossed my mind that you would want to see anyone else. It was quite by accident that I saw you. And I must say I was shocked."

"Are you jealous that I am seeing other men?"

"Hurt, disappointed, saddened, my hopes dashed again, but not jealous. I thought our relationship was everything we both wanted, but seeing you with other men leads me to one conclusion: you're not sure I'm the man you want in your life. I can't understand why you are dating others."

"Because I can," Summer responded.

"That response may fit into your dream, Summer, but it doesn't have anything to do with real life."

"If I promise not to date anyone else, will you stay here, Jack?"

"No. If I have to blackmail you to make me the one and only man in your life, I would never know for sure if I'm the right man for you. You must make that decision without any pressure from me."

Silence filled the room. The two sat looking out the window for some time—thinking, thinking of what could be said or done to reconcile a relationship that had suddenly taken a turn that neither wanted. Someone once said: Two cannot walk together unless both agree. And two people who dearly loved each other were beginning to experience that axiom.

Summer broke the silence. "Please take me home, Jack."

The drive to Summer's home was long and filled with strangeness that neither had ever felt. "My decision to return home in no way diminishes my love for you," Jack explained. "I'm leaving with hope and faith that my overwhelming desire to spend the rest of my life with you will one day come to fruition."

Summer said nothing.

Jack had not expected this response. He had done the one thing he never wanted to do—make her unhappy. That bothered him even more than finding out she was dating other men, and her answer to his marriage proposal.

"I'm not walking out on you, Summer," Jack said as he walked her to the door. "I am giving you breathing space and all the time you need to find whoever or whatever it is in life that you want. I desire nothing but your happiness, even if that means a life without me."

When Jack tried to kiss her goodnight, Summer turned her head. She stood motionless. He hugged her, but she did not hug him in return. Summer seemed as cold to Jack as a rock covered with snow on Grandfather's Mountain.

"I'm sorry I have hurt you, Summer. Please forgive me. I'll call you tomorrow."

As Jack left Summer standing on the porch, he could not hold back the tears. A night he had hoped would bring him everlasting joy had turned into one of grief.

Over the next two weeks, Jack was unsuccessful in contacting or seeing Summer, not even at church where they had both faithfully attended for years. She did not answer his phone calls and emails, or come to the door when he knocked. It seemed as though he had been completely erased from her life. He was heartbroken and could not understand how she could say that she loved him and not even speak to him.

Jack told no one about his misfortune. When people asked about Summer, he merely shrugged it off and said things just didn't work out. But his friends could see the sorrow that he felt.

A still, small voice within reassured Jack that it was time to leave Gold City and start over. There was only one place he wanted to go.

CHAPTER 2

A WALK IN THE WOODS

By the time Jack crossed the Cobbwebb County line, he had pushed all thoughts of Summer to the back of his mind and was thinking about what he would do when he arrived at the home place.

About two miles west of Winston on Highway 46, he came upon a Plymouth Valiant on the side of the road with steam rising from under the hood. He slowed down and stopped in front of the vehicle. Behind the wheel was an elderly lady who looked depressed. He could tell she had been crying.

"Howdy, ma'am," Jack said as he approached. "Looks like you have a small problem."

She stared at Jack for a moment before speaking. "Good afternoon to you, sir. If you are broke and your car is broke, you got a big problem. And that's where I am right now—broke down and broke."

"Well, God sent me here to solve these problems. Open the hood and I will see what I can do to help you get rolling again."

"God has never sent anyone to help me before. And I have never had a white man offer to help me with anything."

"Well that has all changed today. I'm here and I'm going to help you. If I don't, God is going to kick my butt."

The old woman laughed. "You're crazy! I don't believe God would do anything to you if you passed on by me like so many others have already done."

"You're right, ma'am, but I do believe God will hold me accountable one day for not doing what I know I should do. When I saw you sitting on the side of the road I could tell you had a problem, and I had to stop.

"My name is Jack, Jack Porter. What's yours?" he said as he opened the hood.

"Inez Jones is my name."

"Where do you live?"

"Winston. Lived there all my life."

Her problem was what Jack suspected. The top radiator hose had a hole in it. He went to his truck and retrieved his wrenches and in just a few minutes had removed the defective hose.

"You need a new radiator hose, Miss Inez. Do you want to ride into town with me to get a new one or stay here?"

"I don't have any money to pay for a hose, Mr. Jack."

"God has given me the money to pay for this. Are you coming with me or staying?"

"I'll wait."

"I'll be back shortly," Jack said reassuringly.

Ten minutes later Jack came upon a Winston parts store and was surprised to see a familiar face. The parts store manager was Willie Gates, a man he'd served with in the Air Force. Willie retired several years before Jack did and returned to Winston. Jack had lost track of him until now.

After a short exchange of information about family and friends and updating each other on what they were doing these days, Jack purchased a new radiator hose for Ms. Inez's Valiant and borrowed a five-gallon can and filled it with water.

Miss Inez was still sitting in the vehicle when he returned, looking more worried than she had before.

"You weren't worried I wouldn't come back were you?" he asked.

"I wasn't betting any money on it, because I've never had a white man do anything for me."

"Well, today you are getting a blessing from God, delivered through an old white man."

Jack replaced the hose and filled the radiator with water.

"Crank it up, Miss Inez."

She turned on the ignition switch and it cranked right up. Jack watched as the water heated up and began to circulate. As the water level went down, he filled the radiator until it over-flowed, then screwed the cap on and checked the hose connections to make sure there were no leaks. He found none and closed the hood.

Jack advised her to occasionally check the temperature gauge to make sure the car was not overheating. "If it overheats, your thermostat probably needs changing."

"I don't know how to thank you, Mr. Jack. . . ."

"You just did," Jack interrupted. "And don't forget to thank God, because He was responsible for this. It was nice meeting you, and I hope we meet again under better circumstances."

It was close to one o'clock in the afternoon when Jack pulled off the main highway onto West Gate Road, which led to the farms along the Poopah River in Cobbwebb County. He was overjoyed that he had finally returned for good to God's country, the exact spot on the planet where he knew God would dwell if He were to return to Earth as a human. His first stop was to see his brother Mark Porter and his wife Sammie.

Jack and Mark were about the same age. Although Jack had not learned this until much later in life, Mark had come into the family through a different route than himself. When they grew up, Jack never wondered why Mark was about the same age and the only red head in the family. And even to this day Jack was not sure who Mark's real father and mother were. Some said he was the illegitimate offspring of an older sister. Others said that he was an illegitimate child of Jack's father or an older brother. Whoever Mark's father and mother were, the two were brothers when they grew up, and they would remain brothers until the day they died.

When the farms were divided among the children, Mark was treated like all the others in the family and given an equal portion of land. Mark's lot included the old sawmill that had been used to saw timber for building barns, storage sheds, and pens for animals. Mark had retired from the Army after twenty years and returned to the farm, revitalized the old sawmill, and built a comfortable home on the property. To supplement his retirement income, he built a shop behind the house where he worked to make cabinets and just about anything people wanted for their home, yard, or garden. He had been instrumental in assisting Jack remodel the old home place and adding a patio and sunroom off the dining-kitchen area.

When Jack arrived, he found Sammie in the kitchen, where, even at her age, she still spent a great deal of her time cooking and where three generations of Porters could still gather for meals.

"You're one of the last great cooks, Sammie," said Jack. "You can still turn anything you cook into a gourmet meal."

Sammie gave him her loving smile.

"You got it!" said Mark. "The only difference between feeding daddy's hogs and my family is that I don't have to call my family to the table! Anyway, I'm glad you're home, Jack. We've got a few more memories to make yet!"

Mark was glad to have his brother living just down the road. They had many good memories of the days when they had worked on the farm, cared for the animals, and hunted and fished together. They looked forward to adding to those memories.

After a short visit, Jack left his brother's home and drove to the home place. He had sold his home in Gold City and moved all of his household goods to the home place, except for some clothing and a few pieces of memorabilia that he brought along for the ride, including an urn containing his wife's ashes.

It was early November and the weather was perfect for a walk in the woods, and Jack was going to spend the rest of this day doing just that. As a boy he spent as much time as he could in the woods. It was a place of refuge, a world entirely different from the farm. In the woods, there was no garden to worry about, no grass or weeds to pull up, no chickens, mules, or hogs to feed and water, and when by yourself, no one to tell you what to do. In the woods you could stand still, lie down, or sit and feel the calm come over you, feel the peace that overcomes the world. In the forest one could distinctly hear the different sounds of nature: the wind blowing through the trees and reeds, the squeaking of two trees or tree limbs rubbing together when the wind blew, the sounds of the animals and birds—a deer running through the swamp, a fish flopping in the water, a duck flapping its wings to get airborne from the swamp where it had been feeding. Jack's father had always said, "There's never a day that is the same in the forest. You see and hear something different every time you go there." Jack agreed. And he never felt alone in the forest. He couldn't explain it, but he was sure that someone was watching over him. He had escaped too many close calls that could have led to serious injury or death not to believe that.

Jack changed his clothes and put on his boots, knowing that he would need them to reach the river, which was a place where he had brought home many meals for the family. He drove to the far end of the farm. From there he walked along the edge of Bob White Ridge to where the swamp empties into Moccasin

Ditch, which was the route for water entering and exiting the swamps from the Poopah River. As the name implies, one could usually find a water moccasin and a few other varieties of snakes on any given day during the summer.

Except for the pines, the other trees on the ridge and the cypress and tupelo gum trees in the swamp had lost most of their summer foliage, and where the undergrowth was not too thick, one could see for quite a distance. The air was crisp and free of pollution. It had a distinct aroma to it and it was safe to suck it into his lungs. Jack heaved a deep sigh. The afternoon sun, shining through the trees and bouncing off the water in the swamp, gave off an array of colors. It was quiet. It was peaceful. It felt good to be home again in such beautiful and pleasant surroundings. He stood in one spot for some time, just listening and letting it all soak in.

He followed the ridge to the end and crossed a small branch to the ditch that led to the river. The water was normal for the time of year, meaning there was no flooding and any water found in the swamps was from natural rainfall or from previous floods and it had not had time to return to the river. One could tell if the river was rising or falling by the direction the water was flowing in the ditch. Today, it was slowly returning to the river.

Farther along the ditch, Jack stopped again. This time he sat on the trunk of a tree that had blown over. He remembered hunting in this place as a teenager before his dad had sold the timber. The trees all seemed like giants to him then. During his long absence, the forest had once again produced a crop of trees that would soon be ready for harvesting, too.

There will be a day of harvest for me as well, Jack thought to himself.

As he sat on the log reminiscing, a magnificent pileated woodpecker brought him back to the present with its distinct, high-pitched cry as it flew almost directly overhead. No other bird can break the silence of the forest with such a piercing sound. It is a decisive sound, exhilarating to hear, and gives one the impression it is announcing to the world, "I am the king of birds in these parts."

The bird's cry reminded Jack of his feeble attempt to write a poem about a previous experience he had along this ditch.

He had been leaning against a cypress tree looking up and down the narrow banks of the ditch for beaver one fall morning. It was cool, and fog blanketed the swamps. Sunbeams were just beginning to penetrate the forest canopy. Except for the sounds of nature, it was a quiet and peaceful morning.

The loud cry of a pileated woodpecker shattered the silence of the forest, followed by the sound of its pecking away on a dead tree. He recalled the poem this brief moment had inspired, entitled "The Woodpecker," and recited it softly.

> The life and death sounds
>
> Of a woodpecker pecking,
>
> Floating across the swamps
>
> On a misty September morn
>
> Awakens my senses
>
> As a new day dawns

As a boy Jack had heard that sound hundreds of times as he hunted in these swamps and fished in the nearby river. But on this day, the sound of that woodpecker rang out a new message to him about life and death.

The Poopah was quite clear—evidence there had been no floods or rains of late to muddy the water. The air and the smell of the river were different, so much so that if one were blind he could discern that he was near a river.

The sun was sinking toward the close of another day. The hours Jack had been in the woods seemed more like a few minutes. It was time to leave the forest. Enroute to his pickup he spooked a couple of deer and spotted a flock of turkeys. He had given up hunting, but he still enjoyed seeing wildlife in its native habitat.

It was getting dark when Jack pulled into the yard of the home place. It had been a perfect day, and Jack wondered what he had ever done to deserve being so blessed with good health at his age and the ability to return to the place from which he wanted to say his final farewell to the world.

In the back of his mind, he suspected there were some strings attached to his good fortune.

CHAPTER 3

THE CHURCH AT THE FORK
IN THE ROAD

The next morning Jack drove into Winston for breakfast at one of the fast food restaurants where he could always find a few relatives and folks he used to know. After having breakfast with two nephews and a high school classmate, he picked up a few grocery items and headed home.

Not far from the main highway, Jack noticed two black men standing in front of the old church that stood at the fork in the road—the West Gate Road went to the left, and to the right Loop Road took travelers back to the main highway.

At the fork in the road is a great place for a church, Jack mused. *There are just two roads in life: one will take you to places you never wanted to go and the other will lead you to places for which you will be eternally grateful. To get on the latter road one must go through the church.*

The church had been there for as long as Jack could remember. As a boy he had seen people gathering there for Sunday services as he passed by with his parents and siblings during the days of segregation. It was a church where black people worshipped. The church was still active when he entered the military.

It was still standing but looked nothing like he remembered. Back then, the building wore a coat of white paint; picnic tables sat under two huge oak trees, and an outhouse was directly behind the building. There were hitching posts under the oak trees where animals were tied while their owners were worshipping. Now all signs of life were gone along with the white paint. It was obvious from the lack of yard maintenance and the condition of the building that it was no longer in use and of little value in its present condition.

What stood out most in his memory about the church was the name. While most churches have a sign in front giving the denominational name, pastor's name, and times of services, this one had no such sign. The name rested directly over the double-door entryway. Painted in black was a cross, and under the cross in black letters was the word *Church*.

Without even thinking about it, Jack pulled into the churchyard. The two black gentlemen were discussing what to do with the building and the land.

"Good morning. I'm Jack Porter," said Jack as he approached.

"Good morning," they said in unison.

"I'm Pastor Isaias Washington and this is Elder Jeremiah Carver," said the elder of the two.

"Pleased to meet you," Jack said.

"Same here," they replied. "What can we do for you?" the pastor asked.

Jack explained that he had just returned home after an absence of 40 years. "I vividly remember this church from my youth," he said, "and I have always been curious about the name and now I am anxious to know why it has been abandoned."

"What is it about the name you don't understand?"

"I've never seen a name like it anywhere else and I'd like to know the story behind it."

"The cross represents Christ," the pastor explained, "and when Christ and church are placed together what you get is Christ's Church, and if it's not Christ's Church, it's not a church.

"The name cuts across denominational lines and is an invitation to all believers—black and white—that this is a place where one may connect with God and fellow believers."

It was the simplest and best name Jack had seen on any church, and it made for a much less expensive display.

"Were you the last pastor of the church?" asked Jack.

"I was, I'm sad to say. While the building has died, the dream of resurrecting the church has not."

"What happened?"

"Membership declined over the years until it was not possible financially to keep the doors open," Pastor Isaias explained. "So the remaining members joined with their brothers and sisters at the struggling Ark of Salvation Church in Winston. Now the congregation is considering expanding the facility to accommodate a growing membership. However, more than a dozen people who had been members of Christ's Church asked if it were possible to resurrect the old country church under the same name in Winston. That had been the dream of the congregation when they transferred their membership."

Jack didn't want to tell the pastor he had never been inside a black church, but he had the sudden urge to enter this one. "May I go inside the church?"

"Indeed you may," said the pastor. And the trio entered the building.

Even in its best days, the building was primitive. Just inside the entryway were two small classrooms, one on each side. Up front was a small, elevated area for the pulpit and to the speaker's left an exit door. In between was the sanctuary. Six plain glass windows, three on either side, let in light and fresh summer air. The floor, walls, and ceiling were of rough, uneven wood. Toward the front, in the center of the aisle, everything was covered with a thick film, evidence of a wood stove that used to heat the building; a giant hole in the ceiling indicated a chimney. Several wood benches without any backing had been left in the building, along with a couple of wood cabinets. The place was dusty and filled with cobwebs. In a few places rainwater had seeped in through the ceiling and walls and deterioration had set in. There were numerous cracks in the flooring, and there were signs of nature: weeds growing through some of the cracks, mice droppings, and even the skin of a snake. Neither electricity nor running water had ever entered this building.

"How old is this church?" said Jack.

"We don't know the exact year it was built," said Pastor Isaias. "But we have been told this was the first black church built in the county."

"What do you plan to do with the building?"

"We don't know," said the pastor. "It can't be repaired and used again, and I don't reckon anyone would want to spend the money to move it and use it for a barn. I would love to see this church resurrected in Winston, but we don't have the funds to rebuild right now."

Jeremiah said he thought the fire department might want to burn it down as part of their training program.

"I would hate to see something this important to our county's heritage go up in flames," said Jack. "If you would consider giving me the building, I will tear it down and try to sell the timber that can be reused. Any money I receive above my expenses I will return to you and you can use it to start a building fund."

"That's the best offer we've had," laughed Pastor Isaias.

"And the only one, so far," added Jeremiah with a chuckle.

"We will have to see what the church board members want to do, but I suspect they will let you have it rather than see it burned or demolished," the pastor remarked.

"When can you give me a decision?"

"We will make a decision at tomorrow night's board meeting, and we can let you know Wednesday morning," Pastor Isaias said.

Jack gave them his phone number and thanked them for their time. "I look forward to hearing from you," he said as he shook hands again and said farewell.

As he drove home, Jack began to think about what he had just done. *I haven't been home twenty-four hours and may already have taken on a major task. Why did I do that?*

Jack knew the answer to that question as soon as he asked it. Over the years he had found himself in many similar situations. Once again he was simply responding to a call from that small voice from within. And he knew who was calling. He had a feeling something good was going to happen. Besides, he needed something to do to keep his mind off Summer.

CHAPTER 4

THE BOARD MEETING

Pastor Isaias was elated that someone had come along and offered to do something that might get his congregation excited about moving forward with plans to rebuild Christ's Church in Winston. Even though all he knew about Jack Porter was that he had recently retired from the Air Force and moved back to the county, he had done something no one else had: this white man had volunteered to tear down the old church building and try to sell it and give the money to the church, minus expenses.

So when the church leaders met Tuesday night to discuss Jack's offer, the old pastor could hardly believe what he was hearing.

After informing the board of Jack's offer, Pastor Isaias asked for comments, hoping to get someone to move to accept the offer and another to second it and get a unanimous vote to move forward.

But that's not what he got.

"Ain't no white man gonna do something for us for nothing," said one board member.

"Amen, brother," said another.

"He sounds like a con artist to me. He's got something on his mind that ain't good for us."

"Amen, brother!"

"Every time I've had any dealings with white folks who wanted to do me a favor, it didn't turn out in my favor," said another board member.

And the *Amen* brother confirmed it.

The pastor sat at the head of the table shaking his head in disbelief.

"What kind of no good do you think he is up to?" he said.

He got the same response from everyone: "We don't know what he's up to, but we know he is up to no good."

"Just what can this white man do to beat us out of something?" said Pastor Isaias. "We are going to demolish or burn down the building because we believe it is worthless. This man comes along and apparently sees some value in it and offers a helping hand. And we are acting like we want to cut off that hand!"

Until now Elder Jeremiah had been silent.

"Well," he began, "I have some reservations, too, but it's mostly because of what my daddy has told me about things that happened to him in that part of the county. Even the white folks round here will tell you some wild stories about things that happened in that part of Cobbwebb. I'd be willing to bet this man was part of some of my dad's bad memories."

Jeremiah was always telling stories his dad had passed on to him.

"Okay," the pastor chided, "let's hear one of those stories."

Jeremiah explained that his father, Solomon, and his best friend Oscar Williams courted the two daughters of Noah and Abbie Dover who lived about a mile from the Porters. The Porters and Dovers were well acquainted. Solomon eventually married Serena Dover.

Jeremiah told of an incident that happened to his father while he was courting Serena. The story had stuck in his mind like mud on a pig.

"My daddy told me that one Saturday afternoon he and Oscar picked up Serena and her sister Salome and were on their way to Winston when they spotted a suitcase on the side of the road. Oscar was in the back seat and saw it as my dad drove past. He hollered for Dad to stop so he could pick it up. So Dad stopped and backed up the car, and Oscar jumped out, picked up the suitcase, and got back in the car.

"Dad said he thought they had found something of value because it was packed full of something. Rather than waiting until they arrived in Winston, Oscar immediately opened it to find out what was in it."

"What did they find?" the pastor asked.

"Snakes! Dad said he was looking through the rearview mirror when a black snake rose from the wadded up newspapers that had been stuffed in the suitcase to make it look like it was a real treasure trove.

"Dad said he did not have to wait to see what else was in that suitcase. He slammed on the brakes and he and the rest of the passengers exited simultaneously, screaming and hollering."

"I hope no one was hurt," the pastor said as he let out a roar along with the others.

"Thank God they were all okay," Jeremiah added. "But Dad said that he was as close to being scared to death as he had ever been. He said the girls messed their pants, and he did not know if they did just one or both. Standing some distance from the Buick, Dad said they did their best to comfort Serena and Salome while watching the snakes crawl out of the car.

"Dad said the girls would not get back into the car; they walked home. And Mamma never overcame her fear of snakes. In fact, she would not get into a car if it had a suitcase in it, unless it was locked and put in the trunk."

"I've never heard that story," the pastor remarked, still laughing. "How many snakes were in the suitcase?"

"No one counted them, but Dad said there was a bunch of them, and he said they were mad and stunk!"

"How did the girls explain their predicament to their parents?" the pastor wanted to know.

"They told them they had upset stomachs."

"What happened to the suitcase?"

"Daddy took it home and he and Oscar burned it in the backyard."

"Did they ever find out who did it?"

"No, they never did. And I guess it's a good thing they didn't 'cause my dad said he might have done something that he would live to regret. But he was pretty sure it was one or more of them white boys that lived in this part of the county. And Jack Porter lived in this part of the county at that time."

"It could have been somebody who was jealous of Oscar and your dad dating those Dover girls," the pastor suggested. "You've told me many times they were good looking gals."

"My daddy would never have believed that. You ain't gonna find no black man who will play with snakes. My dad said he never picked up anything on the side of the road again, unless it was somebody thumbing a ride that he knew," Jeramiah concluded.

Steering the conversation back toward Jack Porter's offer, the pastor pointed out that this incident happened more than 50 years ago and there was not one piece of evidence that Jack was involved. "Who amongst us did not do something foolish like this when we were kids?" he asked. "When we were kids we acted like kids, but most of us have quit acting like kids now that we are adults. If indeed Jack Porter was a part of this episode in your father's life, I forgive him, and I'm certainly not going to interrogate him about it.

"One of my classmates in Bible College was part Cherokee Indian. He said there was a saying among his people that all honorable men belong to the same tribe. We owe it to Jack and to ourselves to find out if he belongs to that tribe.

"What I'm looking for tonight," he continued, "is your consent for Jeremiah and me to meet with Jack. And after our meeting, if we feel that his offer is sincere, we will extend to him our right hand of fellowship and gratitude for doing something nobody else wants to do."

The board approved the pastor's request without further comment.

CHAPTER 5

MEETING WITH THE PASTOR

Jack was late getting out of bed Wednesday morning, still tired and sore from working in the yard the day before. It was cloudy and cool, so he built a fire in the wood stove, and went into the kitchen to cook some bacon and eggs.

Before he could sit down to eat, the phone rang. It was Jeremiah. Jeremiah asked if he and Pastor Isaias could stop by and discuss the proposal Jack had made to them about the church. Jack gave them directions to his home and planned to receive them within the hour.

Jack ate breakfast, washed the dishes, and made a fresh pot of coffee for his guests. While waiting for them to arrive, he addressed a card to Summer, giving her his new address and phone number. As always, he ended his note with "I love you." He was returning from the mailbox when the two pulled into the driveway. Jack welcomed them and invited them into his home.

Isaias was in his midseventies, Jack estimated, and was the last pastor of Christ's Church. He had been responsible for finding an existing church in Winston with similar beliefs and bringing most of his congregants with him. With the two groups working together, The Ark of Salvation Church in Winston was able to sustain itself and hire Pastor Isaias as its full-time minister.

Jeremiah was an elder in the church and a much younger man—around fifty, Jack guessed. His parents had been members of Christ's Church and he too had some fond memories attending the church as a young lad before it closed its doors.

As Jack poured his guests coffee, Jeremiah asked him if he had been raised in the home they were presently sitting in.

"I was," Jack said, "along with two brothers, a sister, several half brothers and sisters, and a few grandchildren."

After exchanging the usual pleasantries, they gathered around the dining room table to discuss his proposal. Pastor Isaias spoke first.

"I don't want a church I pastored to die before I do," he began. "I have a dream. It is not a dream to change the whole world, but a dream to change the world around me. I want to resurrect that old church at the fork in the road. Even though we have no money, I believe God will bless what we are doing. A lot of people in this county have been touched in some way by Christ's Church. They see it sitting there empty and sinking into decay. If we can get the community behind what we are doing, together we can make my dream a reality."

Pastor Isaias turned to Jack. "How much do you think the wood in that old church is worth?"

It was a good question, but Jack could not give him a definite answer.

"I called a friend in Salem, near the state capital, last night," Jack told them. "He's an artist. I called him because he has contacts in the area and artists use old weathered wood for frames. If I can get a load of boards to Salem before Thanksgiving, it would probably sell at a reasonable price. He advised me that if I were interested in bringing up a load he would alert other artists and we could meet at his home. He could not guarantee me a price, or if anyone would even buy anything, but he felt sure that some of them, like him, needed this kind of wood for frames. The price artists would pay depended on the quality and type of wood."

Jack also explained that some builders use boards from old buildings to spice up certain interior areas of homes and businesses to highlight a particular theme or motif, although he had not had the time to seek a buyer yet.

"I have not done anything like this before," Jack said, "so I can't give an estimate. Let me assure you I am not in this for the money. I would hate to see the oldest black church in the county just go up in flames or turned into rubbish.

"I think there are people who would want to have a framed photo or painting from wood that came from a historic church building. And other mementos could be made from the wood. I'm hoping this will turn out better than we expect. If we make some money to help build your new church that will be a blessing."

"Say, did you know the Dover girls who were raised across the swamp?" asked Jeremiah.

"I sure did," said Jack. "I worked in the fields with them on many occasions. They were beautiful young ladies."

"Serena was my mother," Jeremiah announced.

Surprised to learn of this, Jack wanted to know if she was still alive.

"No, she died of cancer last year and her sister Salome was killed in an auto accident several years ago."

"I'm sorry to hear that. I would love to have seen them again. My brother and I envied those girls," Jack said.

One of the differences between blacks and whites back then was the way they looked at Saturday afternoons.

"We were blessed—or cursed, depending on how one looks at it—with a daddy who believed you could do more work on Saturday afternoon than any other day of the week. And he made sure there was plenty of work lined up for us children to do on Saturday afternoons.

"Our black brothers and sisters, on the other hand, were blessed—or cursed, depending on how one looks at it—with dads that believed Saturday afternoons were close enough to Sunday to make them sacred. And no work was ever planned or performed, unless essential to life, on Saturday afternoons.

"Some of dad's land joined the property of old man Noah and his wife Abbie. Back then their two teenage daughters were blossoming into roses. They were good workers and Dad hired them during the summer to harvest tobacco and chop grass from peanuts and other crops. But they did not work on Saturday afternoons.

"Whenever my brother Mark and I were working in the field next to the Dover home, we noticed that every Saturday afternoon this early 1940s model blue Buick—with a coon tail tied to the radio antenna—came barreling down the dirt road, kicking up dust in its wake. They would pick up Serena and Salome and head out for a good time somewhere. If Mark and I were working in the field, the girls would always wave to us with great delight as they drove past us. Envious of their good fortune, we would wave back, but what we really felt like doing was crying. For two young boys who wanted to be set free on Saturday afternoons, too, it was depressing."

"Thanks for sharing that with me, Jack. Everyone loved my mother. She had many pleasant memories of growing up here, and I'm sure she would have loved to see you again."

Jack smiled. "So have you made a decision on what to do with the church building?" he asked, turning to the pastor.

"For starters, I appreciate your honesty," Pastor Isaias said. "Over the years I have had some white folk make promises they didn't keep. We came here to find out if you are for real, and I think you are. I look forward to working with you and I pray that our relationship will be a blessing to us and our community."

"I take that to mean I can go to work," said Jack, smiling.

"It does," the pastor cheerfully replied.

"I need someone to help dismantle the building," said Jack. "I will be glad to hire someone you know to help me and pay that individual a fair wage from the sale of the wood. And that person can share in the overseeing of all transactions. I will expect the individual to work just as hard as I do, however."

Pastor Isaias said his grandson was looking for work to earn money to go to college. "Tell me when and where you want him to show up and he'll be there," he said.

"Tomorrow morning, 7:30, at the church building. I want to carry a load of timber from the building to Salem Saturday."

Pastor Isaias asked Jack if he would go with him to see the editor of *The Gazette* on Monday. "I'm going to tell the whole world what we are going to do. I have learned that if everybody knows what you plan to do, you can't back out."

"I agree with that," Jack said, "and you will be surprised at the number of people who will give you a helping hand."

He did not say anything to the pastor, but Jack knew Zeb Johnson, editor of *The Gazette*, when he was a reporter for the paper in Gold City, located just outside the main gate to the air base. He was the type of person who believed in bringing the community together and Jack felt that Zeb would support Pastor Isaias in making his dream come to fruition.

Jack asked his guests if they would stay for lunch but both had other commitments. With complete faith in each other, the deal was sealed with a handshake.

After they left, the thought occurred to Jack that the day he returned to Cobbwebb County he was out of dreams. Though he'd dreamt of returning home for some time, he had not thought about what he would do after arriving. *After today's work is done, people need a plan for tomorrow*, he thought. And

Jack could not think of a single thing he needed to do that was more worthwhile than helping Pastor Isaias fulfill his dream. Dreamers do not fulfill their dreams all by themselves, and he suspected that the pastor would need all the help he could get. He had a dream that Jack believed in, and Jack had a feeling it was going to come to pass sooner than expected.

The still small voice told him that.

CHAPTER 6

THE JOURNEY BEGINS

Jack called his friend, Ron Cratt, in Salem and asked if Saturday would be a good day to bring a load of boards for the artists to consider purchasing. After some discussion, Ron agreed. "I'll call everyone I know!" he said. "Anytime between 10 a.m. and 3 p.m. will be perfect."

Jack borrowed Mark's trailer to put the longer boards in. The shorter ones he would put in the back of his pickup. Hammers, crowbars, saws, and gloves were all rounded up and put into the pickup. He was ready to roll when Thursday morning came.

When Jack arrived at the church the next morning he was met by nineteen-year-old Lamont Epstein, a slender, well-built, and handsome young man. Jack introduced himself and told him how thankful he was to have someone to help with dismantling the building.

"You may call me Jack, if you wish, Lamont," Jack said.

"Can't do that," he responded. "My parents taught me to respect my elders. I'd rather call you Mr. Jack or Mr. Porter."

"Mr. Jack will do, then. I don't meet many young people today with your manners, and I must say it's something our society is lacking.

"How did you wind up with a Jewish name?"

"My mother is a nurse. After graduating from college, she moved to New York where she worked for a hospital in Manhattan. It was there that she met my dad, Josephus. Although a Jew, he was not a practicing Jew by faith."

"I gather then that your father is deceased."

"Yes, he died about five years ago of a heart attack. My mother, Melanie, moved back to Winston shortly after he died and we have lived here since then."

"Was he a Christian?"

"I think my dad was a believer, but he never practiced his belief. He was a good husband to my mother and a good father to me and my sister, Naomi."

"What about you, Lamont? What do you believe?"

"At this stage in my life I would have to say that I am a Christian, but I feel like I have some growing to do."

"That's good to hear, Lamont. I don't think Christians ever stop growing. At least, I haven't. We can discuss this more as we are working. Let's get started."

They began taking the building apart in the classrooms, being careful not to remove anything that might cause the building to collapse, or do anything to damage the boards.

It was difficult getting the first board removed without doing any damage to it, but once they had removed the first one, the remainders were much easier to take down. They almost filled the bed of the pickup with boards from one of the classrooms before lunch. That afternoon, Jack decided to work in the sanctuary so they could fill the trailer with some of the longer boards. They filled both the truck bed and the trailer by noon on Friday and tied them down so they would not be blown away during the trip to Salem on Saturday.

Jack observed that the wood in the building was from different types of trees. There were pine, cypress, oak, and a few others that he was not sure of. The boards ranged in length from six feet to twenty feet. Almost all of it was three-quarter-inch thick and a few boards were sixteen inches wide. It looked as though the church had been built with timber left over from other projects.

Left behind in one of the classrooms was a small cabinet with two doors, one that could not be opened and the other broken. It was quite banged up, so the wood was of little or no value. Jack decided to take it home and work on opening the door, just in case something of value was left inside.

Lamont wanted to go with Jack to Salem on Saturday, so they agreed to meet at the Evergreen Motel on the bypass in Winston at 7 a.m.

They were going to find out if their used timber was worth anything.

CHAPTER 7

BEING AT THE RIGHT PLACE
AT THE RIGHT TIME

Jack and Lamont pulled out of the Evergreen Motel parking lot at 7:10 a.m. on a cold but sunny Saturday morning. The road to Salem was four lanes, and not a single traffic light until they pulled off the bypass two and a half hours later.

The Cratts were a good Christian family. Jack had met them through the Christian church in Salem, though it had been many years since they had visited. They were elated to see each other again.

After introducing Lamont, he inspected the load of planks and chose the ones he wanted.

While waiting for customers, Lamont asked Jack why he thought anyone would want the old boards. "When I learned that Ron was an artist, I asked him to paint a picture I had taken of a sail boat on a river in Maine. He framed that painting with boards like these. That painting still hangs prominently in my living room."

It was a pleasant day and made even more so when the Cratts invited Jack and Lamont into their home for lunch.

But at the end of the day, Jack was disappointed in the results of their trip. It was almost three, and their total take was just over $200.00. They had just tied down their load again with straps and were saying farewell to the Cratts when a man from the construction site across the street came over and introduced himself.

One look at Norm Miller and you knew he did not make a living sitting behind a desk. He was middle-aged, muscular, unshaven, and well-tanned from being outdoors, with hands that were used in manual labor; but the way he was dressed indicated he was also the supervisor or perhaps even the owner of the construction company.

He was interested in seeing the load of boards. After careful inspection, he wanted to know what was on the price tag.

Jack explained where the boards came from and what the plan was for selling the old building to pay for building a new church. "To be honest, Norm, we have no idea what the boards are worth, so we are at the mercy of the market and honest buyers."

"Honesty is a word this country has covered up on the dusty floor of capitalism," Norm said. "Is this all you have or are there more?"

"I expect there are three more loads like this, maybe a little more," Jack said.

"How soon can you deliver it?"

"The weather man speaks of rain Monday, so if the weather is fair the remainder of next week, we should be able to deliver by next Friday."

Norm stood for a moment, looking at the planks in the trailer, and thinking. "Tell you what I'll do. I'll give you $5,000 for everything, this load and what you have left. I'll even provide the truck for the rest of the boards."

Jack and Lamont looked at each other—amazed and wondering if this could be true.

"If you want to think about this over the weekend and give me a call Monday, that's okay with me," Norm offered.

"I think your offer is more than generous," Jack replied. "We'll take it."

Norm walked across the street to his pickup, returned with a checkbook, and wrote the first check toward the building of the new church for $5,000.

Norm had one of his workers take them to a nearby warehouse where they unloaded the boards. The warehouse contained a variety of timber, but Jack and Lamont did not see anything like the load they delivered. They did not know if that was a good or bad sign, but they believed they had met a good and honest man and had received an excellent price for the old building.

The gentleman who helped them unload the boards, Mr. Walter Hagan, asked for directions to the old church building. "A truck will be there late Monday and you can begin loading Tuesday," he said. "Here's my phone number. Just give me a shout when the truck is loaded."

Jack and Lamont could hardly wait to get back to Winston to share the good news. A day that seemed to have been a bust turned into one of great joy.

Jack suspected someone was working behind the scenes to make the dream of Pastor Isaias become reality.

CHAPTER 8

SHARING THE JOY

Jack and Lamont arrived in Winston around 8 p.m. They decided to wait until Sunday to give the good news to Pastor Isaias. Jack asked Lamont to present the check.

Jack was up early Sunday morning. He had never been to an all-black church and was eager to find out what it was like. He didn't think there would be much difference between a black service and a white service, but since he had never been to a black service he couldn't be certain.

On his way to church he stopped by to see Mark and Sammie and to return the trailer and invite them to attend church with him. He offered to pay Mark for the use of the trailer, but Mark would not accept a penny. "And I think we'll pass on attending church with you, Jack," he said. "We're not really looking for a new experience."

Jack arrived early at The Ark of Salvation Church. The building was typical of the low-cost evangelical churches erected in the South. It was of modern brick construction, and the sanctuary would comfortably seat 150 people. One could enter the Sunday-school classrooms and restrooms by way of the sanctuary. The podium was on a raised platform located at the end of the center aisle. Comfortable pews were on both sides of the aisle. Directly behind the podium was room for a dozen or so choir members, and behind them on a higher level was the baptistery. Directly in front of the podium was the altar area and communion table. It looked just like most of the other churches Jack had worshipped in all over the world.

While he stood at the back of the sanctuary taking it all in, Lamont and his mother Melanie arrived. Jack was glad to see Lamont for two reasons: he wanted to sit with someone he knew during the service and he needed to give Lamont his money for working the previous week. After meeting Melanie and giving Lamont $200 for his labors, they seated themselves in one of the pews about midway through the sanctuary. Over the next ten minutes, the choir, Pastor Isaias, and two elders—including Jeremiah—took their positions, and just about every seat in the sanctuary was filled.

The 10 a.m. service began with the singing of "All Hail King Jesus." The choir led, and everyone sang. It was uplifting and inspiring. Immediately following, Elder Jeremiah led an opening prayer, after which the choir director led the congregation in three hymns.

After announcements and the offering, the choir gave their rendition of "It Is Well with My Soul," and put more soul into that song than Jack had ever heard. At the end, he wanted to jump up and shout *Hallelujah!* but refrained because he didn't want to make himself any more conspicuous than he already was—he was the only white person in the sanctuary.

Pastor Isaias welcomed everyone to the service and made a point to introduce Jack, informing the congregation of their plans to purchase land in Winston and rebuild Christ's Church.

"Jack has offered to take down the church building and sell the planks. He and Lamont, my grandson, took a load to Salem yesterday. Jack, would you be willing to give us a report on how things went?"

"I'd like for Lamont to come up and tell you what happened yesterday, and he's got something he wants to present to you," Jack replied.

Lamont walked quickly to the pulpit and stood beside his grandfather. As Lamont looked out on the congregation, Jack could tell he was nervous.

"At three o'clock yesterday," Lamont began, "Mr. Jack and I were about to leave Salem without much success in selling the load of boards. But God must have been looking out for us. At the last minute, a gentleman from a construction site across the street from where we were parked came over. After explaining to him that we were trying to sell what we could of the old church building to build a new church, he made us an offer we could not refuse."

Lamont handed the check to the pastor and said, "I'll let my grandfather tell you how much we received for the old building."

The pastor took the check from Lamont and stared at it for a moment and then at Lamont and at Jack. "I can hardly believe what I am seeing on this check," he said. And then he read loud and clear: "Five thousand dollars!" The congregation stood, applauded, and shouted, "Hallelujah! Hallelujah!"

On the way back to his seat, Lamont stopped abruptly and went back to the podium. He asked and was granted permission from the pastor to speak. Lamont looked out over the congregation again, then at his mother and Jack and then began to speak, much more calmly this time.

"I worked with Mr. Jack this week to help remove and load the planks and take them to Salem. Before we sold the building to the contractor, we had made only a little more than $200 on sales to artists in the area. That was hardly worth our trip to Salem.

"This morning Mr. Jack paid me $200 for my labors. That left him seven dollars for his expenses. He has put a lot more into getting this job done than I have, and if anyone should have received $200, it was Mr. Jack. He told me this morning that he would just consider his expenses part of his love offering to the church. As you know, I took this job to earn money to enter college in January. I really need it, but I think Christ's Church needs it more right now."

Lamont took the $200 from his pocket and handed it to Pastor Isaias. "If Mr. Jack doesn't take anything for his labors, I'm not taking anything for mine, either."

Jack was the first to stand and applaud what he had just seen, and the congregation joined in. Jack and Melanie gave Lamont big hugs when he returned to his seat.

When the congregation quieted down, Pastor Isaias wiped away tears and thanked his grandson for setting such an example. "If we are going to resurrect Christ's Church," he said, facing the congregation, "this community is going to have to follow in the footsteps of Lamont. I thank God that I can call him my grandson, and I know God will bless him beyond all expectations for what he has done this morning."

Pastor Isaias's sermon, whether planned or spontaneous Jack did not know, was on the topic of transformation. He said that people had to be transformed from thinking as the world thinks to thinking as God thinks, and used his grandson's self-sacrifice as an example. And though it was an excellent sermon, congregants agreed that Lamont's actions were more powerful than anything that was said.

Nothing good happens in a community until it first happens in individuals, thought Jack. Lamont had opened the door, and Jack sensed that it was going to add fuel to a fire that had already been ignited.

CHAPTER 9

THE INFLUENCE OF A SMALL TOWN PAPER

It was beginning to rain the next morning as Jack and Pastor Isaias entered *The Gazette* office for their meeting with Zeb Johnson. Zeb was an excellent reporter who had turned out to be an even better editor. He had taken over a failing paper and turned it into one of the state's most read and respected biweeklies. His emphasis on community was evident in every issue, and circulation had more than doubled in the five years he had been editor. Zeb loved what he was doing and the community loved Zeb and their paper.

When they arrived at *The Gazette* office, Zeb was in a meeting with the printing press manager. The secretary seated them in Zeb's office, and while awaiting his arrival, Jack viewed the framed news clippings hanging on Zeb's walls. It looked just like his office in Gold City except all the news clippings came from *The Gazette* and the stories of the people were different. None of Zeb's awards for his outstanding work in journalism were visible anywhere in his office. There were no photos of Zeb with any politicians or famous people, although Jack knew such photos existed. Instead, there were stories about people his paper had discovered in the community who had made a difference. His walls were filled with clippings about ordinary people in the community who had made extraordinary contributions to the community.

The article that caught Jack's eye was headlined: "Black Pastor Stands Up for White Man Accused of Killing Two Black Men." That pastor was Pastor Isaias.

The white man in the story was Bud Claymore. The pastor and Bud grew up in the same community and came to know each other while working together for local farmers. They spent time together in the fields, and some of Bud's white friends had resented the fact that he was closer to the black man than he was to them. Bud's family was as poor as Pastor Isaias's and that was probably one of the reasons they were attracted to each other. Had they gone to the same school, they no doubt would have been best friends.

Bud quit school in the tenth grade and became a drifter. He left Winston at age twenty and did not return until he was in his midsixties. He was an alcoholic who worked just enough to support his bad habit. Sometimes he slept on the streets, or in nearby woods, or in his younger sister's garage. He was a quiet man and no one knew the reason for his drinking problem.

Bud had attended a party at a camp on the Poopah River one Saturday night. He got into an argument with two black brothers and made some threatening comments. When the party broke up, he was the last to see the two brothers alive. The next day they turned up missing, and three days later their bodies were found floating in the river.

The district attorney, with nothing but circumstantial evidence and a desire to win black voters, charged Bud with drowning the two men. Not a single person stood up for Bud; the town vagabond had no friends and no money to hire a good lawyer to defend himself.

Pastor Isaias made numerous attempts to persuade Bud to change his lifestyle, but nothing he said or did made a difference.

After the jury was seated and the trial had begun, Pastor Isaias contacted Bud's appointed lawyer and asked to speak on behalf of the accused murderer. This is what the paper recorded from the pastor's comments:

"I have known the accused all my life. He and I worked in the fields together, and I never once saw him kill anything deliberately. He would not even kill a tobacco worm. He would take it off the tobacco leaf and toss it on the ground but would not hurt it. He did not go hunting. He never went fishing. And he told me he ate very little meat. I never saw him hit another individual except to defend himself when he was attacked. I have seen him endure insult after insult but not strike back at his provokers. He has been an alcoholic most of his adult life, yet there is no record of him ever becoming violent or hurting anyone. I want to say to the court that I still love and consider Bud Claymore my friend. But that's not the reason I came; I came to tell you that I know as sure as the sun rises and sets every day that Bud is incapable of hurting anyone, and could certainly never kill another human being.

"If this court should find him guilty on the flimsy evidence listed against him, justice will not be served. When we treat our down-and-out citizens unjustly, just because they are down and out, what will the rest of the world think of us? I beg the court to look at this man as a decent human being who is fighting demons that we cannot see or understand. He has brought more troubles on himself than he can bear. If the court will look closely at this case, I believe you will throw it overboard with the two men who no doubt accidentally drowned in the Poopah River, and free my friend from your jail."

The article confirmed what Jack had suspected about Pastor Isaias—he was and had always been a man of great integrity.

His thoughts about the pastor were interrupted when Zeb entered the room.

"Good morning," Zeb announced. "Sorry to keep you waiting." As he greeted Jack, it became clear to the pastor that the two had known each other for quite some time. "If this man is on your team, you have a winner," Zeb informed the pastor.

"I am proud to say that he is on my team, and I agree with you, Zeb."

"I love your wall decorations, Zeb, and I can tell you the one about Pastor Isaias is a winner. What was the outcome of the trial for Bud Claymore?"

"Three days after the pastor spoke on his behalf, all charges were dropped and Bud was set free. And that is just one story that will tell you why Pastor Isaias is so well respected and appreciated in this community."

Zeb had already heard about what happened at the Sunday service and had assigned a reporter to cover it. Pastor Isaias laid out the plans they had for finding land and raising money to rebuild Christ's Church. Zeb was excited about it because it was a story that connected the present to the past, and a good story because everything about it was good for the community.

He knew there were still racial barriers between many in the community, and he saw this as another opportunity to change that. He believed that the church was the best institution in the community to bring people together. Zeb asked Pastor Isaias to keep him posted on everything that was being done to raise funds, purchase land, or any problems that might arise.

After their meeting with Zeb, Jack and the pastor stopped by Molly's Pastry Shop for coffee and a roll.

After sitting quietly together for a moment, Pastor Isaias spoke. "I'm seventy-five years old, Jack, and I don't know how much longer I will be able to carry on the demanding duties of a pastor. I'm blessed to have Jeremiah and a few others who support my ministry. I'm already thinking about a replacement. Good pastors are hard to find. Many are in it for the money and some have no idea what they are getting into. And the ones in it for the right reason are mostly settled in and don't want to move. Lord willing, I want Christ's Church to be the last church I pastor."

Pastor Isaias was the second pastor of Christ's Church. It had been without a pastor for many years. The former minister served the church for some forty years before retiring. Pastor Isaias pastored the church for more than twenty years and was in his tenth year with The Ark of Salvation.

"I have no knowledge of how the church was started, or the year, but I believe it was in the early 1920s that the building was erected," he continued. "Back then, most people lived in the country and survived mostly off the land. More prosperous times and better job opportunities attracted those who were not big landowners to the city life and better-paying jobs. And that caused the demise of Christ's Church."

"Do you have any building plans?" asked Jack.

"I've thought about it over the years, and I have a vision for what I want done, but I don't have anything on paper. Now that we have started, we will press forward with finding building plans and a site for the church, and come up with how much money we need to make it happen. If we can get most of the money and find a location, we can start on the building project by the end of January," Pastor Isaias said. "How soon will the old building be taken apart and moved?"

"Hopefully, Lamont and I will have that done by Friday."

"How much is the land worth, Jack?"

"I have no idea. You'll have to contact a real estate agency to give you an estimate."

"Sounds like a good idea. I'll do that."

As the two went their separate ways, the rain was falling much harder. Jack sensed that the rain was an omen to what was needed in Winston and many other small towns across America. People needed a cleansing of the soul and a worthwhile dream. Jack was pleased that he had found someone, who, like him, did not want to waste his few remaining years sitting on the front porch. Pastor Isaias had a worthy dream, and Jack was elated that he was playing a small part in helping it come to pass. The additional knowledge he gathered from the article about the pastor added immensely to his admiration of this elderly man of God.

How many Pastor Washingtons would I have met, Jack thought to himself, *had I crossed that black-white line when I entered the Air Force?*

CHAPTER 10

CHRIST'S CHURCH DISMANTLED

Lamont was waiting for Jack on Tuesday when he arrived at Christ's Church. He had arrived early for the day's work, anxious to get started and excited about finishing the job. A large truck was backed up to the front of the building. Inside the cab were instructions giving the location of the key to open the back door for loading the wood, and who to call when the truck was full, or if another truck were needed. It resembled a self-moving van, only larger, and on both sides was the identity of the company—East Coast Builders, Inc.—headquartered in Rockton, just fifty miles from Winston. Jack wondered if Norm Miller was the owner of the company and if he had any ties to Winston.

They were certain the truck would hold most, if not all, the remaining boards. The two men began removing the boards, separating the long ones from the short ones, and putting them into separate piles. When they tired of taking boards off the building, they loaded the ones they had removed to break up the monotony. Except for taking short breaks, they worked until dark on Tuesday.

The Gazette hit the streets Tuesday afternoon, and by Wednesday morning most everyone in Cobbwebb County knew about the dismantling of the church. When Lamont and Jack arrived to continue their work, a few people were already there taking pictures of what was left of the building. People from throughout the county came by, some for photos, and others to watch as the work was being done.

Most of the folks who came to see the church being taken apart were senior citizens, and some had a story to tell. Jack and Lamont listened patiently as visitors recalled important events that had taken place there. Some had met and married their spouse through fellowship in the church, some recalled their salvation experience, and others met lifelong friends there.

One of the older men who came by told of the Sunday when the preacher was working overtime at the pulpit.

"This old man sitting on the front row falls asleep. The preacher begins talking about the great falling away, and the old man falls out of his seat and just lies there on the floor. The preacher thinks he is dead and begins to plead with God that no one has ever died during one of his services and to please don't let it happen today.

"They revived the old man and he was fine, and the service ended there. Some said he was raised from the dead, but he had just knocked himself out when his head hit the floor. It was the most exciting service I attended in this church," the old gentleman recalled.

Jack and Lamont got a chuckle out of that one; it made up for some of the stories that were not so exciting.

The reporter assigned to the story, Zinnia Gregory, came to take photographs and interview both men for another story to be published in Thursday's paper. She brought them a copy of Tuesday's paper, which carried a big headline and a complete story on page one about Pastor Isaias' dream. It was deemed an excellent story and had generated quite a response.

With most of the interior boards removed and loaded onto the truck, Jack and Lamont began to remove the boards from the building's exterior, using Mark's tractor and front-end loader.

They spent the first part of Thursday removing the tin from the roof. The framing for the roof was next removed and then the outside wall boards, starting from the back and working toward the front. With few interruptions, by the end of Thursday they had taken down everything except the studs used for framing and the floorboards.

Not long after the two men started working Friday, more visitors began arriving. Many of them were people who knew either Lamont or Jack. They came by to say hello and chat for a spell or take photos of what was left of the building.

The last things to be placed in the truck were the old benches. Jack kept one of the benches for a memento.

In spite of the interruptions, at the end of the day Friday the work was complete except for the logs that were used for the foundation. Seven cypress logs were originally placed on wooden blocks. When the blocks began to deteriorate, they were replaced with concrete blocks. Some of the wooden blocks were still under the building.

The truck was filled to capacity. That night Jack called the phone number he had been given to let the contractor know the boards had been loaded onto the truck. He explained that everything had been loaded except the cypress logs used for the foundation, and he asked that a log truck be brought in retrieve them. The truck driver agreed to meet Jack on Saturday morning at 8 a.m.

When the two met Saturday morning, Jack was told they did not want the cypress logs; all they wanted were the boards. Jack thought about what he could do with the logs, and it occurred to him that the boards used to build the church were once logs. While it meant more work, he knew the logs could be sawed into lumber and turned into mementos.

Jack would need his brother's help once again, and he was confident Mark would oblige. His sawmill could not handle forty-foot logs, and Jack had no way of moving logs that big without hiring someone who owned a log truck. So Jack cut the logs in half. Once again he borrowed Mark's trailer and front-end loader to load and haul the logs. Since the church was located only a few miles from his house, the job was not too difficult. He and Lamont cut, loaded, and hauled the logs to Mark's sawmill before dark on Saturday.

The cypress logs would create more work for Jack, but he didn't mind because he believed they were more valuable than the timber they had sold to Norm Miller.

CHAPTER 11

THE COMMUNITY RESPONDS

Jack felt sore and exhausted as he crawled out of bed Sunday morning. He wondered if nineteen-year-old Lamont felt the same way. His job at the air base had not required the use of so many muscles, and it certainly did not require that much physical labor.

He met Lamont and Melanie at the church door before the 10 a.m. Sunday service to make sure they found a seat. They entered the sanctuary and sat near the center once again and read the bulletin while other worshipers piled in. He looked around the sanctuary and saw two other white families present. The pews were filled and extra chairs had to be placed along the aisle; they too were filled by the time the service began.

Following the announcements, congregational singing, and the special offering for Christ's Church, the choir sang "He's Got the Whole World in His Hands." Jack had never heard a choir with so many magnificent voices, and their rendition of this Negro spiritual moved the audience to give them a standing ovation. And for some reason, the song resonated deep within his soul. *Even this remote part of the world, overlooked and underappreciated*, Jack thought, *is in His hands*. Just as he had the week before, Jack felt the presence of God in this place.

When Pastor Isaias stepped up to the pulpit, he was as excited as Jack had seen him since they met. He gave a glowing report of how the local paper had spread the word about their plans. "People have been stopping me on the streets and calling me on the phone," he said. "Some," he continued, "gave me encouragement and offered to pray for the work, and others wanted to know how to make a monetary contribution. Some even gave me money on the spot, which I placed in the special offering this morning."

Before preaching, Pastor Isaias called Lamont to the podium. Lamont was surprised that he had been singled out, because he didn't have anything to give this Sunday. Pastor Isaias told the congregation that the main reason so many people had come forward was due in part to what Lamont had done the previous Sunday. "His sacrifice, though small, touched the hearts of many in this community and people have responded in ways that I never imagined.

"I received a call this week from the President of Cobbwebb Community College. She told me that an anonymous donor had paid the full tuition for one year for Lamont." That brought a round of applause from the congregation. In addition, the pastor presented Lamont with five $100 bills for books and miscellaneous expenses from this same generous individual. That led to another round of applause.

Lamont was stunned and speechless. After a moment's pause, and with tears in his eyes, he said, "I'm overwhelmed and grateful to the person who gave me this gift and I promise that I will not disappoint that person or others who have placed their faith in me."

"That's not all, Lamont," the pastor added. "The manager of the Dixie Distribution Company has offered you a part-time job beginning immediately."

Lamont was all smiles when he returned to his seat. "I can't believe this is happening to me," he whispered to his mom.

Pastor Isaias gave what was considered yet another profound message on the importance of relationships: with God, with neighbors, with classmates, with coworkers, "with all the people we come in contact with. We need each other," he said, "and if we are not connected, we cannot work together to better ourselves or our community."

Before closing the service, the pastor announced: "We will have two worship services beginning next Sunday, an early service at 8:30 a.m. and the regular service at 10:30." This was a first for the church, a sign that bigger things were about to happen.

After the service, Jack asked Lamont and Melanie if he could take them out for dinner, and they accepted. Jack took them to a popular family restaurant located in the country near the town of Grassland. Grassland was more like a rural community, but nevertheless, it had its own high school and mayor. Some called it the garden spot of Cobbwebb County.

The Dodge City Steak House, according to the county Chamber of Commerce guide to area businesses, was the only one in the community and was rated among the best in the eastern part of the state. The family-owned-and-operated business, the guide noted, was started by retired Marine Sergeant Major J.R. Sampson. Ms. Goldie Pletcher, chamber director, called J.R. "a genius. He began small," she said, "and just kept adding to it, and over the years turned it into a restaurant and family fun center worth more than a quarter million dollars."

Jack and Melanie chose the Western-style beef spareribs while Lamont ordered the Texas burger with hot peppers and fries. While enjoying their meal, Jack asked Melanie what it was like being the daughter of a pastor.

She was grateful her dad was a pastor. "I know many others who were children of pastors that would not say this. Mom and Dad did not have to drag Hannah and me to church. We looked forward to it every Sunday. Our parents expected us to do what was right, not because we were the daughters of the pastor, but because that was the right thing to do. Our parents never expected any more from us than they did from all the other members of the congregation or anyone else they knew. 'Being a responsible, law-abiding, and honest member of society,' Dad would tell us, 'has nothing to do with being a Christian. That was simply being a good citizen. And if you are a good citizen, you will enjoy being with others who are, especially in a Christian environment.'"

"Pastors do not make much money, so how did you get your degree in nursing?"

"By the time Hannah and I graduated from high school, Mom had joined the work force. My parents made great sacrifices to put me through school. I also worked part-time and was lucky enough to get a couple of scholarships. I was broke when I graduated, but I did not owe anyone anything, except my lasting gratitude to my parents. I had no problem getting a job."

Their mother was affectionately called Ms. Cecily by members of Pastor Isaias's congregation and her friends. She was the fifth of seven daughters born to the Swanson family that lived on East Gate Road, a house that Jack had walked past many times to catch the school bus. If Jack's memory had not failed him, all seven of the girls were tall, slender, and very attractive.

"My mom is also a very good pianist," Lamont volunteered.

"That's great to hear," Jack said. "Maybe she will play for Christ's Church when it is rebuilt in Winston."

"Do you really believe Dad is going to see that building erected?" said Melanie.

"You bet he will," said Jack. "Your dad's faith runs deep; that church will be completed next year. Lamont started something two Sundays ago when he put that $200 he earned for college into that offering plate. All a fire needs to get started is a little spark, and Lamont was that spark. I think you are going to see the community come together like never before. Pastor Isaias is doing something that unites us. And this community needs more unity, and people are beginning to see that."

"I don't believe it will happen next year," Melanie said. "You need at least $100,000 to make it happen, and all we have right now is $5,200 plus whatever was collected this morning."

"You gotta believe," Jack said, smiling. "God works in mysterious ways; just watch over the next few months and you will see what I mean. And if that church is open for worship by the end of June, can I tell your dad that you are his pianist?"

"This is one time I hope I'm wrong," Melanie laughed. "But if that building is open for worship services by the end of June, you can tell Dad that I'm his pianist."

It was a pleasant afternoon spent with people Jack had already grown fond of. Melanie and Lamont thanked Jack for treating them to dinner, and they went their separate ways.

Jack was listening to WINS, Winston's only radio station, when he turned onto West Gate Road. Louie Armstrong was singing one of Jack's favorite songs, "What a Wonderful World."

Jack's new world was wonderful, but there was something missing that would make it even more so. Summer was still very much on his mind.

CHAPTER 12

HOW MUCH ARE OLD CYPRESS LOGS WORTH?

The first order of business Monday was to finish cleaning up the debris on the Christ's Church lot. The tin had to be carried off to the scrap yard, the glass from the windows and the concrete blocks had to be disposed of, and the old blocks that had been left under the building had to be removed or piled up and burned.

In the process of completing these chores, Lamont and Jack found a few old coins that had apparently fallen through the cracks in the wooden floor. They had found three or four while removing the flooring.

On a hunch, Jack later borrowed a metal detector from a nephew and searched the area thoroughly and found several other coins, some buried in the soil and others near the surface. He didn't know much about the value of old coins, but he would investigate that later.

By the end of the day, the lot was cleared of all debris and ready for market.

What to do with the logs was the next question. On Tuesday, Jack called Pastor Isaias to inform him that the lot was ready for sale and asked for a meeting to discuss how to use the logs to raise money to build the new church. Pastor Isaias invited Jack to his home for lunch.

"If you are not having chitlins today, I'll be there," said Jack with a chuckle.

"We ain't eating no chitlins," he assured Jack.

The pastor lived in a modest three-bedroom home in a part of town that included a mix of white and black families. It was representative of the changes that had occurred in towns throughout the country. After Pastor Isaias lost his wife to cancer, his oldest daughter, Hannah, remained in the home to care for him. She was gracious and pleasant to be around and an excellent cook. Her vegetable soup and turkey sandwiches were delicious. She served cherry pie for dessert.

After lunch Jack and the pastor went into his study to discuss another way to raise money for the building project. Jack laid out his plan.

"I think we can saw the cypress logs into boards, then turn the boards into mementos and sell them. How would you like to have the word 'Welcome' on a board from the oldest black church in Cobbwebb County hanging beside the entryway to your home where guests could see it?" Jack asked.

"Sounds like a good idea to me," said Pastor Isaias.

"My brother is very good at making things out of wood. I believe he could take those boards and make desk name tags, signs to welcome people into their home, or put family names on boards that could be placed in the home or entrances to homes.

"I think people would be willing to pay a little extra to help build the church, especially when they are getting something they can use that is made from the first black church in the county. It would be a treasure they could pass on to their children and grandchildren."

"How much would each memento cost, and how much will the church get from each?"

"I think we should sell each item for the same price. I need to discuss the price with my brother and find out what he wants for his time and expenses."

"How much do you think the church would get from the sale of the mementos?"

"I can only give you a guess. If we can use all the boards, I believe you will get several thousand dollars. If we could get them on the market after Thanksgiving, they would make excellent Christmas gifts, and I believe they will sell quickly."

"Sounds like a wonderful idea, Jack. I'm not going to wait to bring this before the board. I'll tell them what we are doing. You have my blessing to begin immediately."

Before leaving, Jack went to say farewell to Hannah.

"What are chitlins?" she asked.

Jack laughed. "There was a time when that was soul food, but by your response I think we can add chitlins to the list of things we used to eat but don't anymore. Chitlins are the small intestines of hogs."

"You won't have to worry about getting any of those at this house!"

He thanked her again for the splendid lunch and departed.

CHAPTER 13

A BROTHER COMES TO THE RESCUE

When Jack hauled the cypress logs from Christ's Church to Mark's sawmill, he failed to tell his brother what his plans were. He was not taking his brother for granted, but Jack was betting everything that Mark would come to his rescue. And Jack did not have a backup plan.

Jack felt that Mark was the best brother anyone could ever hope to have, but Mark was not a born-again believer. He was a good man. He would do anything to help a neighbor. But his visits to a church were business only. He would go to attend a wedding or the funeral of a friend or family member. He acquired all of his biblical knowledge simply by watching those who professed to be a Christian. And because of what he had seen in some of those professing Christians, he had chosen not to be a follower of Christ. His brother could discard the bad apples from a barrel and keep the rest, but when it came to the church members, in Mark's eyes they were all bad apples.

Mark professed that he believed in God and that all was well between him and his Maker. He had written his own plan of salvation and was counting on God to accept it. Jack didn't agree with his brother's thinking, but in Jack's eyes, it was no different than churches that had interpreted the Scriptures to fit their beliefs.

After discussing his plans for using the boards from the cypress logs with the pastor, Jack went to see Mark and found him cleaning up his carpentry shop, which included every tool needed to build cabinets for homes or offices and any ornament one could design for decorating the home or yard. Bird houses, bird feeders, quilt racks, welcome signs, and desk name plates were among customer favorites, and just about everyone in Cobbwebb County had something in their home or yard that Mark had made.

"How's my favorite brother, today?" asked Jack.

"Since I'm the only living brother you have, that's not much of a compliment," Mark laughed.

"Yeah, but if they were all alive I would still say that."

"To be that kind to me on a Monday morning, you must want me to do something for you."

"Well, as your brother I consider it my duty to keep you busy. That way, you will stay out of trouble and it will keep you active so you will live longer."

"Some days I feel like I have already lived too long, Jack."

"I know the feeling, Mark, but once I get to moving each day, I begin to feel better, and if I am doing something worthwhile, I feel even better."

"I take that to mean you want me to feel better and you already have a worthwhile project lined up to make that happen, right?"

Jack was glad his brother was in a good mood.

"Yep, I do, and not just for you, but for us."

"It wouldn't have anything to do with them cypress logs, would it?"

"I think you saw me coming before I arrived."

"I did. And don't forget, I'm your brother, and I know you as well as you know yourself. What is it that you want me to do?"

"That's the question I've been waiting for you to ask," Jack replied with a big grin on his face.

The brothers sat on nail kegs and Jack began to explain what he hoped to accomplish with the logs once they had turned them into boards.

"The first question you want answered is why I am involved in helping a black church. All of my life I have been involved with the church, but never before have I been involved in one that is predominantly black. When I retired and moved back home, I decided that I was going to get out of the rut I had been in for years and try something new.

"There has always been something about that church at the fork in the road that has appealed to me. Maybe it is the memory of driving past it on Sundays to get to another one two miles down the road simply because of the color of our skin. Before I even had the opportunity to attend an all-black worship service, I found myself in front of the old church talking to the former minister and another gentleman. To my surprise, I discovered that it is the oldest black church in Cobbwebb County.

"You and I and the rest of the family have passed that church on many a Sunday, but we never gave a second thought to stopping there to worship with them. This was in the days when blacks and whites didn't do anything together but work.

"Things between the races have changed some since I left here, but when it comes to blacks and whites worshipping together, things are about the same. If we believe in the same God, why can't we worship Him together? God does not look at our color but at our hearts. If the heart is not right with God, you are not of God. It's that simple.

"I got involved because the old church was going to be burned or demolished. I saw some value in the old building and offered to do what I could to sell the timber. Money raised from the old church building is being put in a savings account toward the resurrection of a new church building in Winston.

"When I agreed to try to sell the timber in the old building, I had no idea what it was worth, or if we'd get anything. I just believed that God would bless what I was doing, and He has not disappointed me. The boards from the building sold for $5,000, and we still have fourteen 20-foot cypress logs that are as good today as they were when the building was constructed.

"Once we turn the logs into boards, I am asking you to turn them into mementos that can be sold to people who would gladly pay a reasonable price for something that was once a part of the oldest black church in the county.

"And there's one good reason we should do this. When you and I were kids, we pulled some dirty tricks on our black brothers and sisters. It's a wonder someone didn't die of fright when they opened that suitcase. This is a chance to do something that is good, something we can tell the world about and not be ashamed of."

"You make it sound awfully easy, brother."

"Sawing up the logs is the easy part, and you and I can do that," Jack explained. "But making the mementos from the boards would require some assistance, and I believe I can round up volunteers to do that. All you would have to do is supervise the volunteers who would do the work here in your carpentry shop."

"How much of my time are you asking for?" Mark asked.

"Two weeks at the most."

"Exactly what do you want to make?"

After brainstorming for an hour, the brothers were pleased with what they had come up with:

- A three-piece cross: twelve inches high with a six-inch cross, mounted on a six-inch by four-inch board. *Church* would be etched into the wood at the base of the cross.

- A two-foot by four-inch board with the word *Welcome* etched into it.
- Desk nametag, fourteen inches by three inches.
- Family name: example, The Harpers, with the first names of each family member below it. Etched onto a twelve-inch by five-inch board.
- A combination hat and coat rack. A three-foot by four-inch board with five pegs for hats or coats.

Each item would be identified on the back with *Wood from Christ's Church*. To make sales simple, the price for each item was set at $13.00.

"What are you getting out of all this work you are doing for the church, Jack?"

"Satisfaction, brother. Satisfaction."

"A man can't live on satisfaction."

"That's true, Mark. However, I can always sleep on satisfaction."

"Well, I think my time and the use of my equipment and facilities are worth something."

Jack did not try to persuade his brother to do the work for free, since he was not affiliated with the church.

"How much do you want?" Jack asked.

"I really don't know, since I have not done anything like this. What do you think it is worth?"

"Does a thousand dollars seem reasonable to you?"

Mark paused for a few seconds before answering.

"Well, I guess that sounds about right."

"Do you want the money up front or after the job is finished?"

"We'll settle after the project is completed."

Jack asked Mark to produce one each of the items. He wanted the pastor to show them to church members and to Zeb

Johnson. Zeb said he would publicize the project in *The Gazette*. The plan was to have the items on the market around Thanksgiving, which was two weeks away.

"I can do that, but we have to saw up the logs first. And if you can get me some volunteers, we can begin production Monday."

"How many do you want working with you at one time?"

"At least three and no more than five, and I would like to work from 8 a.m. to around 5 p.m. If we have to work at night I will, but I would rather keep normal hours."

With the plan in place, Jack was confident it would be completed on time and produce more than just money for Christ's Church.

CHAPTER 14

THE BLIND MAN

Jack and his brother worked Tuesday afternoon, Wednesday, and part of Thursday sawing the logs and smoothing the boards. The logs produced 94 one-inch thick boards, varying in width from four to six inches.

Jack wanted to be the first to own a memento from the old church. He sawed off an end piece from one of the largest logs. It was one-inch thick, about fourteen inches high, and eighteen inches wide. After smoothing it on both sides and sanding it around the edges, he had his brother burn into the piece of wood the words: *An old man lives here with his memories.*

Jack hung the memento beside the front door of his home. He stood there for a moment admiring this piece of art. Memories from his childhood surfaced along with his last contact with Summer Brown. The memento would remind him of happy and sad times. *It's a part of life,* he thought, *and without experiencing both I wouldn't know the true meaning of either.*

Around one thirty Thursday afternoon Jack pulled into the parking lot at Cobbwebb Community College, a new and much needed addition to the county since Jack had left. It was nothing fancy, but locals considered it a godsend to students who wanted to pursue a trade or receive their first two years of college credits at a reasonable price.

He made his way to the information desk and asked for directions to the carpentry shop. The receptionist was polite and gave him the information he needed.

The carpentry program at the college was in a separate building, complete with all the machines and tools needed to teach the trade. The instructor's office was located in one corner of the rectangular metal building, and the rest of the concrete floor space was filled with machines and students working on a variety of projects. Mr. A.J. Tinsley, the instructor, was going from work project to work project, checking on what the students were doing and making sure no safety rules were being violated. He spotted Jack when he entered the building and came over to meet him after making his rounds with the students.

"What can I do for you?" Mr. Tinsley asked. They shook hands and Jack introduced himself.

"Please to meet you, Mr. Tinsley," Jack said.

"Same here. And please call me A.J. You look like your building days are over, so I'm guessing you're not here to sign up for one of my courses. What can I do for you?"

They went into A.J.'s office and Jack explained what he was doing to help Pastor Isaias.

"I'm looking for volunteers to help with a project to raise money for the rebuilding of Christ's Church," Jack explained. "They will be working with my brother Mark. If we can get enough volunteers, we can complete the project in a few days."

"Is your brother the one who makes all those things I see in yards all over the county?"

"That's him."

"I've seen a lot of his work, but I've never met him. He's very good at what he does."

"Thanks. I'll pass your compliment to him when I see him again."

"Great! So, exactly what do you want me to do?"

"Talk with your students and see if they will volunteer to make the mementos. They can work around their class schedules and perhaps you could give them some extra credit for the training they will receive making them."

A.J. looked out the window for a moment and then at Jack. "I don't know if I want to get involved again with anything associated with the church."

"I take that to mean you were once involved in the church."

"I was. My wife and I went to church every time the doors were opened."

"Do you have any children?"

"No, and I don't have a wife anymore, either."

"I'm sorry, A.J. I hope I'm not opening old wounds. And I certainly didn't come here to pry into your private life."

"That's okay, Jack. Since my wife and child died two years ago I've not had anything to do with the church."

A.J. paused for a moment as he looked down at the gold wedding band on his ring finger.

"Leona and I had been married for five years before she finally conceived. Five months into the pregnancy something went wrong. They tried to save the baby by performing a C-section, but she was born dead. Then Leona died two days later of complications from the surgery. I always believed she died of a broken heart.

"I've tried to get over it, Jack, but as you can tell I haven't. God did not answer any of my prayers, and I blame Him for everything. Maybe I shouldn't. Anyway, that's why I'm not excited about getting involved with the church again."

"I'm sorry this happened, A.J. You have shared with me something very personal, and I appreciate that as well as your honesty. I wish I could say something to comfort you.

"I don't know how I would have responded to a similar situation, and I thank God that I have not had to suffer through a tragedy such as yours.

"When my family and I lived in Salem we became disenchanted with the church and we too blamed things that happened on God."

"What happened to cause you to get involved in the church again, Jack?"

"I spent half a day with a man who was dying of cancer. He was one of the most extraordinary people I've ever known. I've never forgotten Bob Dale. Although dead, he's still speaking to me."

"What did he say to you?"

"I had heard of Bob because he was one of the most popular people in the area. His parents dropped him off at the state capitol when he turned eighteen and left him. That would not be a big deal to me, but it was to Bob. He was blind. All he had was an extra change of clothing and a few dollars in his pockets. The Salvation Army took him in and helped him get on his feet. He spent the rest of his life in the capital city. He made his living as a vendor, selling snacks and souvenirs around the capitol building and the downtown area. He loved everybody and everybody loved Bob.

"I met him through my next-door neighbor who asked me to sit with him one Saturday morning. At that time, Bob was in the hospital dying of cancer. Someone had to stay with him around the clock, and he had plenty of friends who gladly obliged. My neighbor had an emergency, and that's why she asked me to fill in for her.

"To answer your question, Bob didn't say anything to me. It was what he did that morning that penetrated my heart.

"I arrived at the hospital around 7 a.m. and Bob was still asleep. He woke up about nine and I introduced myself and let him know that I was there as a replacement for my neighbor. He acted as if he had known me all his life and thanked me for coming. He was happy and seemed to sense that he was leaving this world soon and was just waiting for an angel to come and pick him up in a chariot.

"I helped him get out of bed and to the bathroom. I helped him wash up and put on a clean gown. He was not hungry but asked me to get him some coffee while he sat up in bed.

"While we were doing this he sang a song that I first heard at a Salvation Army service in Germany. The title of that song is "God is So Good." It didn't mean much to me when I sang it with the congregation in Germany. But when Bob sang it I could not hold back the tears. This dying man sang the song as if God were sitting in the room listening!

"The next day my wife and I were in church. And we have not missed a Sunday since then unless we could not go because of weather or sickness.

"I never saw Bob again. He died that Monday and was buried on Wednesday. If I'm able, I hope to sing that song just before I die. I'm persuaded that God arranged for me to spend that Saturday morning with Bob.

"I hope I have not taken up too much of your time, A.J."

"No, you haven't, Jack. That's quite a story. Thanks for sharing it with me."

"I would be grateful if you'd think about my request over the weekend and call me Monday with your decision." Jack gave him his phone number.

"Sure, I'll do that."

As Jack left the campus, he couldn't help but sing the song that Bob sang that Saturday morning, because he believed that even in the worst of times, God is still good.

CHAPTER 15

UNSWEETENED TEA

When Jack entered The Ark of Salvation Church on Sunday, he was focused on finding volunteers for the memento project. He had prayed that A.J. would at least speak with his students about helping, even if he did not want to get involved. If they didn't volunteer, he didn't have a backup plan.

He found Melanie and Lamont seated in their usual pew and joined them. Melanie always had a smile for him and today she gave him a hug, which took his mind off his search for volunteers.

The songs for the day were all among Jack's favorites and he found the pastor's message positive and spiritually uplifting. Jack felt the whole service had been prepared just for him, and thus the time seemed to pass quickly.

As the choir sang "Give Me Thy Heart," Pastor Isaias extended the invitation. "The altar is open. Come and give your burdens to the Lord," he pleaded.

Jack was surprised but elated to see A.J. Tinsley walking down the aisle. He too went to the altar, put his hand on A.J.'s shoulder, and knelt beside him. The two remained for some time before A.J. stood up.

"Thanks for coming to the altar with me, Jack. If you have the time, I'd like to talk with you about those volunteers you need."

"Let's get something to eat," Jack suggested. "You name the place and I'll pay for lunch."

"I can't turn that down, although I'd be glad to pay the bill."

A.J. chose a small mom-and-pop café on the west side of Winston, near the Poopah River. A.J. knew the family and told Jack that he ate there often to help keep them in business.

While eating their barbecued chicken dinner, A.J. said he had decided to support the memento project.

"I'm elated to hear that and I know Pastor Isaias will be too," said Jack. "Something tells me that you did not come to church this morning just to see me. I hope this is a sign that you are going to try to move beyond the loss of your wife and child."

"It is."

"May I ask what has caused this sudden change?"

"Our conversation got me thinking about how I have responded to my tragedy. But what really got me moving was something that happened last night over dinner. My brother and his wife have been my biggest supporters since Leona and our child passed. Without them, I don't know where I'd be today. I dearly love those two people. Once a week I'm invited into their home for a fellowship meal.

"My brother's wife is a great cook, and she goes out of her way to make it special just for me. They don't drink tea, but she knows I love sweet tea so she makes some just for me every time I go there for a meal.

"Last night she forgot to put sugar in the tea. I hate unsweetened tea. It's bitter. But I drank it anyway, and I didn't dare say anything about it. As good as she has been to me, I didn't have the heart to complain about such a trivial matter. I drank all of it because I didn't want her to discover that she had forgotten to put the sugar in it.

"It made me realize that everyone has to drink a little bitterness sometimes. My sister-in-law loves me and would never deliberately give me anything that is bitter. If my sister-in-law would not do anything to harm me, how can I believe that God would? For the past two years my life has been stuck in the self-pity and 'blame God' mode, like a 45 RPM record playing the same thing over and over. It's time I moved on. Beginning today, I'm asking God to help me become the person I used to be."

Jack was mesmerized. He had witnessed a miracle. He knew God was the mastermind of the sudden change he had seen in A.J.'s life.

A.J. said he would speak with his students Monday and assured Jack they would want to be a part of the memento project.

"By the way, who was the woman you were sitting with in church Sunday?"

"She's the pastor's daughter, Melanie. Her husband is deceased. Her son Lamont was sitting with us."

"Now I have a favor to ask, Jack."

"You want me to introduce you to her, right?"

A.J. smiled. "I've got to start living again. And I want someone to share my life with. She looks like a good prospect."

"If you return for the evening service, I'll gladly make that happen. I'll also introduce you to the pastor and his other daughter, Hannah."

Jack had begun the day wondering what he would do if A.J. did not assist in securing volunteers for the memento project. Now, he was in awe at what God had done with a glass of tea, without the sugar!

CHAPTER 16

A LESSON IN GIVING

Monday was a busy day for Jack. All of A.J.'s carpentry students volunteered to support the memento project. Jack met with A.J. and his brother Mark and worked out a schedule for them to produce the mementos.

He had lunch with Pastor Isaias and Hannah and presented them with the form he had designed for memento orders and his plan for promoting the sale of the mementos.

"You have my blessing, Jack."

"Great! Now I need a volunteer to receive and process orders."

Without hesitating, Hannah spoke up. "I'll be glad to take care of that!"

After lunch Jack went to see Zeb Johnson. Zeb was happy to see Jack and receive an update on what was being done to raise the money for the new Christ's Church building.

Jack showed Zeb the order form and asked if he could print 200 copies while he updated him on plans to sell the church foundation logs to help build the church. "Of course we can! I'll get my secretary right on that," said Zeb. "And let me get Zinnia in here to take some notes while you show me those items."

Zeb was amazed at what was being accomplished with an old dilapidated church building. "Usually buildings like this are burned or bulldozed into a pile and left to rot," Zeb said. "This one has become a rallying cry to do something that is worthwhile and important to our community. I wonder how many other buildings we have destroyed that could have produced similar results. Has anyone placed an order yet?"

"No. We plan to start taking orders after the Sunday morning worship services at The Ark of Salvation Church. Since some of the people who worship there are the last surviving members of Christ's Church, Pastor Isaias thought this was the appropriate place to start."

Jack offered to give Zeb any or all of the items being made from the church timber for his support.

"I appreciate your kind offer," Zeb said. "But I cannot accept it. I get paid for what I do, and I do what I do because I believe strongly in bringing unity, brotherly love, and the spirit of working together to make good things happen, things that make all of us better people. This project does all of those things, and I want to do more than just write about it. I want to be the first person to purchase all five items.

"I might not be there Sunday," he continued, "so I want to complete the form now and give you the money. To whom do I write the check?"

"Christ's Church," Jack said. "And the cost for all five items is $65."

Zeb made out the check and handed it to Jack. It was for $100.

"You've given me $35 more that we are asking, Zeb."

"I know. Sometimes good things don't happen because we fail to do more than what is required. You are a long way from raising $100,000. If we all give just a little more, I believe it will happen."

Jack could only say *Praise the Lord* for that kind of thinking. As he drove to the church to drop off the forms, he remembered what his former boss had said about Cobbwebb County. *We might not be located in the prime time world,* Jack thought, *but you won't find better people anywhere on the planet.*

CHAPTER 17

FLOODED WITH ORDERS

A copy of the order form was placed in Sunday's church bulletin, and almost every family in attendance submitted an order for one or more items. Jack counted the number of each item ordered so his brother would know how many of each was needed. Production of the mementos began early Monday.

That afternoon, Pastor Isaias brought a complete set of mementos made from the wood of Christ's Church to *The Gazette* office and presented them to Zeb Johnson. Zeb was not the type of person who wanted to see his picture in the paper, but he made an exception in this case. On page 1 of Tuesday's edition was a photo of Zeb receiving the mementos from Pastor Isaias along with a story about turning the foundation logs into boards used to produce them. A copy of the order form was printed on page 3. And Zeb endorsed the project on the editorial page.

> *By now most residents of Cobbwebb County are aware of the vision Pastor Isaias Washington and his congregation at The Ark of Salvation Church have of bringing back to life the oldest black church in the county.*
>
> *Christ's Church was located in the fork of West Gate Road and Loop Road. About 10 years ago, when it could no longer support itself because of dwindling*

membership, the doors to Christ's Church were closed and the remaining members became a part of The Ark of Salvation Church in Winston. Their goal then and now is to rebuild Christ's Church in Winston. That vision lay dormant until a few weeks ago.

The Ark of Salvation Church has grown to the point that two Sunday services are now needed to accommodate worshipers. Rather than expand the sanctuary, Pastor Isaias and the former members of Christ's Church decided it is time to resurrect the old church in Winston.

The final chapter on the old church building is now being written. It has been taken apart, board by board, and sold to a contractor. The cypress logs used for the foundation have been sawed into boards and these are being used to make mementos, which are being sold and the money placed in a bank account for the new Christ's Church facility. Most of the work has and is being done by volunteers.

Pastor Isaias says it will take at least $100,000.00 for land and church construction. He doesn't even have the land yet and only about $10,000.00 has been raised thus far. As with any project of this size, there are believers and non-believers.

Your county newspaper stands with the believers. This is not just an effort to rebuild Christ's Church. This church is an important part of our heritage and we need to preserve it. And as we join in this effort, we are bringing our community closer together, making it stronger and better than ever. Who could possibly be against that?

This is one project that will make all of us winners. We at The Gazette office hope our readers will stand with us in the believers' corner.

The Gazette hit the streets of Winston Tuesday afternoon, and those in the county received their copy Wednesday morning.

Hannah Washington's phone began ringing Tuesday afternoon and did not stop for two straight days. She received more than 100 phone orders, enough to keep Mark and his college students busy for two more days. Thursday morning's mail brought in sixty-seven more orders, more than enough to keep the volunteers busy Friday.

Mark and the student volunteers made 497 items, filling all the orders received through Thursday. And most of the wood from the cypress trees had been used. Mark decided to work Monday to fill any additional orders.

Jack called Hannah and asked her to quit taking orders, and then he promptly informed *The Gazette* of the project's success.

More orders were received in the mail Friday. All the remaining boards were used Monday, and all but nine orders were filled. Jack asked Hannah to hold off on calling those whose orders could not be filled. He wanted to wait and see how many more orders would arrive by mail.

By Thanksgiving all the orders had been either picked up or mailed, and $10,954 had been raised from the project. Like Zeb, many people gave more money than was necessary to purchase one or more of the mementos.

Thanksgiving was Jack's favorite holiday. He had much to be thankful for and was looking forward to counting his blessings with family and friends.

CHAPTER 18

THE HIDDEN DRAWER

After five days of eating too much and spending time with family and friends, Jack was ready to finish the memento project and send thank you notes to the volunteers.

Hannah had quit taking orders by phone, but a few more had arrived by mail. Counting the nine that had not been filled the previous week, Jack now had in his hands seven more. The sixteen orders were for a total of twenty-six items.

Jack did not like the idea of turning down anyone, so he decided to call Norm Miller, the building contractor who purchased the boards. It took several calls before Jack got through to Norm, who was well aware of the work being done to raise money to build Christ's Church. He agreed to give Jack the boards on one condition: Norm would place the final order. Jack could not turn that down. Jack took his order over the phone, which raised the number to seventeen and increased the total number of items to thirty-one.

Mark and the volunteers were more than willing to do what was necessary to finish up the project. "I think we can complete this in a day," Jack said. They all agreed Thursday was the best day.

On Tuesday Jack went to see Pastor Isaias to give him a report on what he was doing to close out the memento project and to suggest he personally deliver the mementos Norm Miller had ordered.

"Norm has a vested interest in Cobbwebb County and might be a good candidate to build the church facility," Jack told the pastor. "I recommend discussing this with him after you present him with the mementos."

"Great idea, Jack. Please arrange a meeting with him. And I'd like for you to go with me."

Pastor Isaias told Jack that he had a buyer for the land on which Christ's Church was located, but the deed to the property could not be found. "Apparently it was never filed with the Register of Deeds Office in Winston," he lamented.

"What happens if the deed cannot be located?" said Jack.

"I don't know. I guess we will have to hire a lawyer to find out."

When Jack drove his pickup into his garage he noticed the old cabinet that he had picked up from Christ's Church. For some reason he had forgotten about it. One of the doors would not open, and he was curious to know if there was anything inside.

At one time, the three-foot-high cabinet had two doors that opened from the center with hinges on each side. It did not have legs, but just sat flat on the floor and was about three feet wide and eighteen inches or so deep. The right door was missing, but the hinges were still in place. The bottom of the left door had been pushed or kicked inside the cabinet. Nothing was visible inside. Jack removed the hinges rather than use a hammer to burst the door loose.

To his surprise, Jack discovered a small drawer affixed to the underside of the top of the cabinet. It could be seen only after the cabinet door was opened. With little effort, Jack opened the drawer. Inside was yet another wooden container. Jack examined it on all sides, and nothing was written on it, but when he opened the lid he discovered three things inside: a deed, a logbook, and a quill.

Jack did not try to open the deed or the logbook. They had been well preserved inside the two boxes, but they were dry and he did not want to open them for fear they would crumble from a lack of moisture. He decided to put them in an open place for a few days where they could absorb moisture naturally before examining them. And he decided not to say anything about his find until he knew for sure what he had.

To take his mind off the deed and logbook, Jack spent the next two days cutting firewood for the next winter. As a boy he had cut wood and sold it for spending money.

While the work was physical and far more tiring than it was when he was young, Jack did not notice because his mind was on two of those items in the box. He was itching to find out what the deed had to say and what was written in the logbook. Every time he went into the house he checked on them, but he kept his vow not to open them until Saturday.

Thursday morning Jack picked up three students from the college and took them to Mark's carpentry shop. Mark was waiting for them when they arrived. By 1 p.m. they had completed all the orders. Jack wrote out a check to his brother for $1,000 and thanked him again for the use of his facilities, machines, and his labors. He treated the students to lunch before taking them back to the college and delivered the orders to Hannah for distribution, all except the one for Norm Miller.

Before finding the box, Jack thought his involvement with Christ's Church would be finished on Thursday, except for the meeting with Norm and the pastor.

It was wishful thinking.

CHAPTER 19

FINDING LOST TREASURES

Jack's feet hit the floor Saturday morning before the sun came up. The last time he was this excited upon waking was on his wedding day and when his children were born. He didn't even eat any breakfast, just had a glass of orange juice. He retrieved the deed and logbook from the laundry room, where he had left a window partially open to let in fresh air—exposing the logbook to natural moisture—and sat down at the dining room table to inspect them.

The deed was signed by all parties on February 7, 1920. The land, "two acres more or less," the deed stated, was sold to Christ's Church for $1.00 an acre. The seller was Hump Bell, a farmer who owned the land adjacent to the church property.

Jack next opened the record book. On the first page was a drawing of the cross and beneath it the word Church. Page 2 contained information about the sale of the property to the church.

Beginning on page 3 was a list of the people who had provided some of the materials needed to build the church. As Jack read through the list he was astonished at how many people in the community, both black and white, had contributed to building the church in some way. He was surprised, too, because he had never heard his dad mention giving anything toward building the church, and yet among the contributors was "W. F. Porter – seven cypress logs and twenty-four oak blocks." He either knew or was familiar with most of the names of white people who were on the list. The sign outside his front door and the mementos he had from the old logs meant a lot more now to Jack because they had been a gift to the church from his dad.

The church was constructed over a period of eighteen months, with the first service being conducted in July 1921. The logbook noted that forty-nine people attended the first service.

In the next section of the logbook were the names of the charter members of the church. A church member served as the first pastor until one was hired years later. After the list of charter members, the names of others who became members of the church were listed.

Jack surmised that the deed, logbook, and quill had been left by someone who had been keeping the records and suddenly died, and that no one else knew about it, and so they had been left to fate.

Although hungry, Jack could not wait any longer to call Pastor Isaias and tell him the good news. He didn't want to tell him over the phone, so he figured out a way to get a free breakfast.

When Jack called, the pastor wanted to know why he was so privileged to hear from him at 8:30 on a Saturday morning.

"I've called to make a deal with you," Jack answered. "If you can persuade Hannah to cook me some pancakes or eggs and sausage, I will bring you some news that is almost too good to be true."

"Hannah!" Pastor Isaias shouted, "Jack has some good news to give us but we have to feed him to get it. Can you cook him some pancakes or eggs and sausage for breakfast?"

Jack heard her response: "Be glad to," she said.

After a quick shower, Jack gathered the two boxes and headed for Winston. He arrived at the pastor's home a few minutes after nine. He could smell the sausage cooking before he entered the home. After the usual greetings, they decided to eat breakfast and then discuss the good news.

After eating the best breakfast he'd had since returning to Cobbwebb County, Jack began his story with the cabinet. "I have no idea why I decided to keep it," Jack told them. "One door was missing and it was not something I wanted to keep for any particular reason. I guess I am somewhat like my dad. He never threw away anything."

Pastor Isaias and Hannah listened intently as Jack told them about the drawer inside the cabinet and how it had been attached in such a way that one had to remove the door to discover it. Then he took the drawer he had brought with him from the paper bag and placed it on the table. And then he opened the box found inside the drawer and retrieved the deed to the property and gave it to the pastor.

Pastor Isaias and Hannah were awestruck. "Praise the Lord! Praise the Lord!" they said simultaneously. "I can cancel that appointment with the lawyer Monday," the pastor exclaimed.

Jack gave him the logbook. They did not recognize all of the names of those who had contributed building materials, but they were amazed that the whole community, black and white, had come together to make possible the building of the church. The church membership brought tears to the pastor for he had known many of them who were now deceased. He knew the struggles they had endured and remembered their dedication in their final years.

Jack and Hannah sat and listened as Pastor Isaias told stories about the last days of Christ's Church and its members. "They pulled together, cared for one another," he said, "and held on until they could not hold on any longer. We all wept when we held the final service in that old building. And we all vowed that we would not let Christ's Church die. The sermon I preached that final Sunday was from Chapter 37 of Ezekiel. Ezekiel had a vision of dry bones being raised from the desert, symbolizing the return of God's people to Jerusalem. It came to pass. And I know that Christ's Church will rise again. I just hope I live long enough to see it happen," he cried.

Jack was deeply touched. With a heavy heart, he placed his hand on the pastor's shoulder and told him, "It will happen, brother, and you will get to preach again in the new building."

"I'm keeping these treasures in a safe place," the pastor said. "They will be part of that new church building, something to remind future generations of our heritage."

Jack thanked Hannah for a delicious meal and gave her and Pastor Isaias big hugs as he left for home. His mind still on his visit with the aging pastor, Jack had not noticed how beautiful the day was until he turned off the main highway onto West Gate Road.

He was going to spend the rest of this day enjoying the quiet and beauty of the forestland he had inherited from his dad.

CHAPTER 20

EAST COAST BUILDERS, INC.

Jack had one thing on his mind Monday morning when he awoke: schedule an appointment with Pastor Isaias and Norm Miller, the CEO and founder of East Coast Builders, Inc., headquartered in Rockton.

After breakfast he decided to see if there was anything on the Internet about Norm Miller or his company. From the order for the mementos, Jack knew that Norm was married and had two sons and a daughter. That, and his suspicion that Norm was a successful builder, was all he knew. His search was successful. The history of the company and a brief biography of Norm Miller were included in the web address under the company name.

Jack was surprised to learn that Norm was a graduate of Grassland High School, the smallest and best school in the county. He got his engineering degree from Carolina State University and began his career as a builder. Over the next twenty years he built a booming construction business. The value of the company was not given, but Jack knew that any company with more than 200 full-time employees was a successful company.

After reviewing the information about Norm and his company, Jack was convinced that he was the man to call on to build Christ's Church.

After scheduling an appointment with Norm, Jack went to the church to see Pastor Isaias, who had just returned from seeing the real estate agent about the sale of the old church property.

Pastor Isaias invited Jack into his office. "I've got an appointment for us to see Norm Miller at 1 p.m. tomorrow in Rockton," Jack announced. "If that is not a good time for you, I can reschedule it."

The pastor looked at his calendar. "Tomorrow is a good day for me. What time shall we leave?"

"Eleven a.m. That will give us an hour to drive there and an hour to have lunch before the meeting."

Jack shared the information he picked up on the Internet about Norm Miller.

"Well," said Pastor Isaias, "that's quite a revelation to me. Him being from here and a builder, he just might be someone who could take on this building project once we get the funds."

"Exactly my thoughts, too," said Jack. "After you present him with the mementos, let's find out if he is interested in building the church, and if so, get a feel for what it will cost. How much money do you have in the building fund?"

"I can hardly believe how much has been raised and contributed. If we get $12,000 from the sale of the church property, we will have around $50,000."

"Wow! Where did all that money come from?"

"From everywhere; people from all over the state, and some from out of state, sent love offerings. I'm proud to say that our own members have given quite a bit, too, but we are all amazed at the amount of money that has come from people who used to live in the county or have relatives who live here. If we had the land to build on, I think we could begin construction soon. We don't have to have all the money up front. We could borrow some."

"Have you found any property you'd like to build on?"

"We've seen a couple of places we'd like to build on, but there are no "For Sale" signs, so we are still looking."

"You've been blessed in raising the money, so I'm sure the good Lord will find a place for you to build on."

The next day Jack gathered the mementos for Norm Miller and picked up the pastor and headed for Rockton. He took his camera in order to document the presentation.

En route, Pastor Isaias revealed some of his thoughts and feelings about himself and what had happened over the past few weeks.

"I've been a pastor for more than fifty years," he began, "and I've never experienced anything like what I am seeing now. I can't explain it. God is doing a work through people I would never have expected Him to use."

"What do you mean by people you wouldn't expect God to use?" said Jack.

"Well, it started with you, a total stranger. We're getting ready to tear down or burn the old church building and you come along. You are the first white man to ever reach out across that black-and-white dividing line and offer to help. And in spite of what you said at the beginning, you have not taken one dime for your services. I haven't seen that before, not even from my black brothers.

"I was about to give up on rebuilding Christ's Church until you came along. As things started happening, I began to realize that the world around me has changed more than I thought. An old white man helping an old black preacher fulfill his last dream! If you'd walked down the same road I've walked down all these years, you'd know that what I am experiencing is nothing short of a miracle.

"Where there were doubts and darkness just a few weeks ago, now there is hope and light. I see a church being resurrected where all of God's children can gather to worship and honor Him. My hope is that we can do away with black churches and white churches and just have churches. I know that will take a while, but everything has a beginning, and I pray that Christ's Church is the beginning for the people of Winston."

"I'll say amen to that," Jack interrupted.

Pastor Isaias continued, "When I left Cobbwebb County some fifty years ago, I had no plans to return, other than to come and visit my family and friends. But when Christ's Church began to fade away, my mother persuaded me to return. Like the Scripture tells us to do, I honored my mother and returned. She knew the church would not survive out in the country, and she knew the old church building was not worth preserving. So she made me promise to keep it alive by building a new sanctuary in Winston. Shortly thereafter she died of a heart attack or a stroke one night in her sleep, with a smile on her face.

"Following her passing, we had to shut the doors to Christ's Church, and the last twelve members and their families placed their membership with The Ark of Salvation Church in Winston. My mother died and the church shut down, but her dream became my dream and that has never died. And when we rebuild Christ's Church, my dream of having a church for all God's children will be passed on to the next generation. God's people are all connected, even in their dreams."

"Yes, I believe we are, too," said Jack.

"The logbook you showed me Saturday was a surprise to me in two ways. The first surprise was that my mother had kept that logbook. Her name was not on it as the author, but I know her handwriting, and that's how I know she kept it. The second surprise was that I had no idea how many white folks had contributed to building the church. If we can build one together, we should be able to worship our Creator together."

Jack agreed with the pastor again and offered to do all he could to persuade white people to come and be a part of Christ's Church.

"I want to thank you, Jack, for all you have done. I thank God that I can call you a friend and a brother in Christ."

Jack was touched. He had not sought nor expected such accolades, but he was grateful that what he had done had sparked a revival of the pastor's dream because he believed in it as well.

"Thanks for sharing that with me, Pastor Isaias, and I want you to know that I feel the same about you. You are a pillar in this community, and I admire you for what you have and are doing."

Before they arrived in Rockton, Pastor Isaias spoke of Lamont's sacrifice. "That inspired me, too," he said. He was quite amazed also at how the college students and Mark Porter had gotten together to make the mementos. "I've never had so many white people give me donations and encouragement to resurrect this church. And the local paper has been a blessing. That's why I know that the time has come to turn my mother's dream into reality."

After stopping for lunch, they made their way to the headquarters of Norm Miller's construction company. His office was located in one of the city's older buildings. It had been upgraded to meet the needs of a construction company.

Norm was waiting for them when they arrived. After introducing Pastor Isaias, Jack retrieved the mementos, and the pastor presented them to Norm and expressed his appreciation for purchasing the timber from the old church building and giving some of the boards back to finish the memento project. Norm was grateful for the mementos and promised they would be prominently displayed in his office and home.

"What are your plans for building the church?" said Norm.

"I'm glad you asked," said the pastor, "because all we have right now is a dream and money enough to begin moving forward. Have you built any churches?"

"A few," said Norm.

"Would you be interested in building this one?"

"It would be an honor. I have constructed a few homes in Cobbwebb County, but I have not built a church there."

Pastor Isaias and Norm discussed details about the size and shape of the building, the lot, the sanctuary, classrooms, and baptistery.

"Since you are a native of our county, it is our desire that you build it," Pastor Isaias said. "If you will consider working with us, I'd like to have you come up with a building plan and present it to our congregation, along with an estimated cost."

"I'll be glad to," said Norm. "I'll have one of my architects work directly with you on the plan. We should have one ready by the first of the year."

It was a good meeting. Pastor Isaias was more excited than ever about fulfilling his commitment to his mother.

He was quiet and reflective on the trip home. About the only thing he said was, "We've got to find some land to build on."

"Christmas is just around the corner," said Jack, "and maybe Santa will surprise you with the land you need."

Pastor Isaias laughed at the thought. "Be nice if he would, but I'm not counting on it."

"There *is* a Santa Claus," Jack admonished.

CHAPTER 21

A BROTHER'S CONFESSION

About two weeks after the memento project was finished, Jack's brother Mark came to visit him one night after supper. Normally when Mark went out at night his wife accompanied him. On this occasion he was alone. Jack did not think much of it. He was just glad his brother had come to visit him.

Soon after Mark arrived and they had exchanged pleasantries, the two men retired to the living room.

After some small talk about family and the upcoming holidays, Mark became serious.

"I've got a confession to make," he said.

Puzzled, Jack said, "About what?"

"The memento project. I've been thinking a lot about what you said."

"What did I say?"

"For one thing, about them pranks we pulled on some of our black neighbors. I'd hate to think what would have happened had someone been hurt or if they had found out who was behind them. I'm just grateful that nothing bad happened."

"I think God was looking out for us, Mark."

"But that's not the real reason I came here tonight. You said something about sleeping on satisfaction. I'd never thought about that before. But I have since you gave me that check for a thousand dollars. I have not been able to sleep on that money."

Mark reached into his shirt pocket and pulled out the check and handed it to Jack.

"I'm not going to cash this. Please forgive me for taking it in the first place.

"Our dad helped to build the first church. You are helping to build the new one. At my age I don't need the money as much as I need the sleep and peace of mind.

"No one has ever asked me to do anything for a church. Thanks for asking me. I've learned some things from this experience that have made me a better person."

Deep down, Jack had believed his brother would return the check. Even so, sitting and watching his brother make the confession touched him deeply. Mark had done nothing wrong, and he had every right to expect something in return for his services.

Jack was witnessing something he had longed to see in his brother—a transformation, a rebirth into understanding that there are some things money cannot buy. His brother had moved from watching what was going on in the community to being a part of what was going on in the community.

Jack had always been proud to call Mark his brother, but never more so than at this moment.

He went to Mark and told him that, and gave him a hug. And for the very first time in his life, he said to him, "I love you, brother. And I thank God for you."

Mark did not respond with similar words, but he did not have to. They were both in tears.

CHAPTER 22

A REPORTER COMES FOR AN INTERVIEW

The week before Christmas, Jack was transferring wood from his pickup to the storage shed behind his home when Zinnia Gregory appeared.

"I rang the doorbell, Jack, and then I heard noise out back. I'm glad I caught you at home."

"Good morning, Ms. Zinnia, and welcome. I had my mind on preparing meals and Christmas shopping and didn't hear you drive up or ring the doorbell. You're just in time to help unload this wood!"

She laughed. "Good morning to you, too, Mr. Porter. And please call me Zinnia."

"It's a deal only if you call me Jack."

"It's a deal then!"

"What have I done to deserve a visit from such a distinguished member of our community?"

"I've been assigned to do a story on Jack Porter."

Jack looked at her with a big grin on his face. "What you really mean to say is that you don't have any real news to write about so you are going to make up some, right?" said Jack.

"Well, news is like beauty. It's in the eye of the beholder. And Zeb Johnson and I have the same news eyes and we think you are good for at least one story."

"Only one story!"

"Well, that's all for now."

Jack didn't really see himself as the subject of a story, but he couldn't turn down a young, single, and very attractive young lady. He had read all the articles she had written about the efforts to resurrect Christ's Church and considered her an excellent reporter, a rare jewel in a rural community.

"I know you are not from around here," said Jack. "I'm curious to know how a talented young lady like you wound up here."

"There's not much to tell. I grew up in the District of Columbia. My parents struggled to help me graduate from Carolina University where I earned a degree in journalism. When I graduated, there were too many journalism applicants and not enough jobs. I took the job with *The Gazette* more than two years ago because I needed a job and it was the only one I could find at the time. My goal is the return to D.C. and work for one of the dailies there or for a national magazine."

"What do you think of this part of the world?" Jack asked.

"This interview is going in the wrong direction," she declared. "You are not writing a story about me, are you?"

Jack laughed. "No, but I could if I worked for a newspaper. Like you said, news is in the eye of the beholder, and I think your presence in this part of the world would make a great story.

"You don't have to tell me what you think of this part of the world, but I would like to know why you were named Zinnia."

"I'm sure you have already guessed. My mother thought zinnias were the most beautiful flowers in the world, so she named me Zinnia."

"Your mother did a good job of naming you. If I saw you among the flowers, I'd have to reach in and pluck you right out," Jack said as he smiled at her.

Zinnia blushed and looked at the ground. "Thank you for that compliment, Jack, but can we proceed now with me asking the questions?"

"You wouldn't want to interview an old man on an empty stomach, would you?"

"There you go again, asking the questions."

"Well, I'm being honest with you. I'm hungry, and when I'm hungry my mind seems to focus on food. Have you had lunch?"

"No, and before you ask, I don't have time for lunch with you today. I have another appointment. Were you raised in these swamps, Jack?"

"Yes. Why do you ask?"

"I've heard a lot of people talking about the swamps and swamp people. I've never seen a swamp, except from my car as I drive past them. And I can't see much from the highway. Would it be too much to ask you to show me a swamp? I'd like to see for myself if what others tell me is fact or fiction."

"It would be a pleasure to do that, Zinnia."

"How long will it take?"

"We can do the interview and tour the swamps in about half a day."

"May I call you before I come out next time?"

"Please do. Just make sure to leave me a message if I'm not at home. When I retired, I gave up all my weapons of mass communication except the home phone."

Zinnia laughed.

"What shall I wear?"

"Something comfortable and warm, and bring your tape recorder so you won't have to worry about taking notes. And don't forget the camera. I want to take some photos of you."

"There you go again. Don't forget that I'm writing the story and taking the pictures, too," she admonished.

You've gotta love a gal with her spunk, Jack thought to himself.

Zinnia hadn't even left the driveway, and Jack was already looking forward to her return. He knew she was in for a real treat, as he liked nothing better than educating people about the *Beautiful and Bountiful* parts of Cobbwebb County.

And that, he thought to himself, *is a better story than she could possibly write about me.*

CHAPTER 23

THE PREACHER IS SURPRISED AGAIN

Jack's sons, their wives, and four grandkids came to see him over the Christmas and New Year's holidays. The weather was cold and wet, but no snow fell, which they all considered a blessing since it made traveling much easier. They attended the early worship service at The Ark of Salvation Church and Jack was surprised to see several other white families present. Pastor Isaias and the choir combined to give another uplifting and spirit-filled service.

The bulletin that morning noted that the Christ's Church property had been sold, and that funds for the new church now stood at $62,351.50.

Lamont Epstein and his mother Melanie were there for the early service, and so was A.J. Tinsley, the carpentry program instructor from the college. Jack had promised A.J. that he would introduce him to Melanie but had forgotten all about it until this moment, so after the service, Jack made good on his promise. After introducing the two, Jack made it a point to praise A.J. for the great job he was doing teaching carpentry to students at the college and for his part in getting volunteers for the memento project.

Melanie seemed pleased to meet A.J. "I've heard about the work you do at the college. Thanks for helping with the project to raise money for Christ's Church. And it's good to have you worshipping with us today. I hope you will be back next Sunday."

A.J. was elated. "You bet I'll be back next Sunday!"

The weather was extremely cold the first week in January. Jack thought about going to Florida to visit a friend, but it was cold in Florida, too. So he stayed home and kept the fire going and caught up on his reading. He thought about fixing up the old pew he had kept from Christ's Church, but that was as far as he got. It was just too cold to do anything outside.

Jack thought about Summer. He had sent her a Christmas card but had heard nothing from her, and he had called, but no response came. He could only assume all was well, but still he wondered about her.

The boredom that had set in was broken when Pastor Isaias called.

"I've got some unbelievable news!" he announced.

Jack had not previously heard that much excitement in the pastor's voice, not even during one of his sermons.

"A white man about your age came into my office this morning and offered to sell us three acres of land for a dollar an acre! Can you believe that?"

"Hallelujah! I told you there was a Santa Claus!"

The pastor continued, "At first I just wanted to grab him and give him a big hug. Then I thought, *I'd better find out if he's trying to sell us three acres of swamp land!*"

"That was good thinking," Jack laughed. "Where is the property located?

The pastor went on to explain that the man had taken him to the property. "It's located on the back side of the Oakdale Subdivision," he said, "in a low-to middle-income housing development. The tract of land is on a hill high enough to protect the property from the Poopah River when it occasionally overflows its banks. It's the perfect place for the church! I drove past it when we were looking for land, but there was no "For Sale" sign on it. You've got to go and look at it for yourself!"

Jack wanted to know if there were any zoning restrictions that would prevent a church from being built on the property.

"I can't answer that, but it is a good question and I will find out."

"Who is the giver of this wonderful gift?"

"He introduced himself as Will Webster, but I don't know his full name."

The name sounded familiar to Jack, but he could not put a face to it. Of course, he did not know very many people in Winston because he had not attended school there.

Jack thanked the pastor for sharing the good news with him and offered his assistance if he needed it, promising to go and look at the property.

As Jack began to settle back into his melancholy state, he remembered the year that he had boarded a train in Rockton for Lackland Air Force Base in Texas. He had taken the oath of office in late December and was put on leave until after the New Year's holiday before reporting for duty. There were four people from Cobbwebb County who had enlisted at the same time, but Jack had forgotten their names and faces.

Since the name Webster had seemed to resonate with Jack, on a hunch he decided to go through his military records and see if he was among those on the orders. Jack had retained a copy of every order he had received during his Air Force career, and he kept them in the order they were received in a three-ring notebook. Finding the order would be easy, but searching through boxes and boxes of keepsakes to find the notebook took a while. By the time Jack did find the notebook, he vowed that he would never criticize his dad again for not throwing anything away.

Jack opened the notebook and right there in the front was the first written order he had ever received, telling him where to report, when, and to whom to report. Farther down on the page were the names of the four Cobbwebb County boys who had pledged their allegiance to protect the United States against all enemies, foreign and domestic. The names were listed in alphabetical order and Jack's was just above "Webster, Marcus W.," who was last on the list.

Could this Webster be the same one who offered to sell three acres of land for three dollars to Pastor Isaias? Jack wondered.

He was going to find out.

CHAPTER 24

DISCOVERING SANTA

Jack looked in the telephone book and found a Marcus W. Webster. He dialed the number listed. There was no answer and no answering machine.

With nothing better to do, Jack decided to clean house. It was not his favorite thing to do, but he could not stand living in a house that was dirty. In the process of making his home presentable, Jack ran across the coins he and Lamont had picked up while taking down Christ's Church. He had cleaned them the best he could with soap and water, stored them in a coffee cup and left them on the dresser in his bedroom. He couldn't remember why he had put them in his bedroom. Perhaps it was because things he had put aside for another day were easier to find there.

That night Jack called the Webster home again. Still no answer. He'd try again in the morning, and he decided that if he did not get an answer he would visit the home. He needed to go to the library in Winston anyway. He wanted to do some research on the value of old coins.

After breakfast on Saturday Jack called the Webster home again. Still no answer. Jack suspected that the phone number had been changed, so he wrote down Marcus' address and hopped into his pickup and headed for Winston. The sun was out and it was warmer than it had been all week. It felt good to get out of the house.

Jack knew where Plantation Drive was located, so it did not take him long to locate Marcus' home. The driveway was empty, but he could see a vehicle in the two-car garage. Jack rang the doorbell and waited.

After a couple of minutes an elderly man in pajamas and a robe opened the door.

"Good morning," Jack began and introduced himself. "I hope I am not bothering you too early in the day."

"No, no," the gentleman replied. "What may I do for you?"

"Forty-one years ago this month, three other young men from Cobbwebb County and I departed the train station in Rockton for Lackland Air Force. I have reason to believe that you were in the group."

The man looked at Jack somewhat amazed and said, "I was in that group of men, but I couldn't pick a one of them out of a line up today if my life depended upon it."

"Your name then is Marcus W. Webster and you go by Will. Is that correct?"

"Since you know so much about me, why don't you come in Mr. . . ."

"Jack Porter, and please call me Jack."

Once inside, they shook hands and Will confirmed that he was the man Jack was looking for.

"What made you decide to track me down? If I remember correctly, we played penny ante poker all the way to Texas. I don't owe you any money, do I?" said Will as he let out a little chuckle.

"No, and I don't think I owe you any either. Pastor Isaias Washington called me yesterday and told me an elderly white man had offered to sell him three acres of land for a dollar an acre. As you know, funds are being raised to rebuild Christ's Church and the pastor has been looking for suitable property.

When I asked him who the man was, he said 'Will Webster.' He was ecstatic about your offer.

"I admit," Jack continued, "that your name did not ring a bell at first. But for some mysterious reason the name stuck in my mind. So just on a hunch, I pulled out my Air Force records and there on the first set of orders you and I received were our names. In a town the size of Winston I didn't believe there could be two Will Websters. I tried calling twice yesterday and again this morning but did not get an answer so I assume your number has changed."

"It has and I'm glad you made the effort to track me down," Will confided.

For the next two hours the two men exchanged life stories, beginning with the day they stepped off the train in San Antonio and began walking down different roads that did not meet again until this reunion.

Toward the end of their meeting, Will wanted to know why Jack had gotten involved in helping the black community rebuild Christ's Church.

"When I was a boy," Jack began, "my family attended a church two miles down the road from Christ's Church. As I look back on that, I know now that my parents, like most others of that day, had put an invisible curtain around the black community. And if you were white, you could not go on the other side. The yellow bus that transported me to school went another mile down the road to deliver me to an all-white school, driving right past the black school. The restaurants I ate in were divided, blacks on one side and whites on the other. Blacks sat in the balcony of our theaters while whites occupied the seats below.

"A great deal has changed since then, but you and I know that in many of our towns the one place where blacks and whites should be sitting side by side is the church, but that has not happened. I don't know why. But when I moved back to Cobbwebb County last year, I came determined that I was going to reach across the color line to my black brothers and sisters whenever I could. And God put me to work the day after I returned.

"I'm curious to know why you gave three acres of prime real estate to Christ's Church."

"I'm not a practicing believer. My deceased wife was, and she raised our two daughters in the church. But I have had little to do with the church, black or white.

"My daughters left Winston after they graduated from college and married. They and their husbands have good jobs and are happy where they are. I purchased the three acres of land many years ago hoping that our daughters would settle here and build homes on the property. But that is not going to happen.

"They were home for the holidays and heard that Pastor Isaias was seeking property on which to rebuild Christ's Church. We got to talking about what I should do with the property and both of my daughters suggested that I sell it to Pastor Isaias.

"When I quizzed them on how much I should ask for the land, both gave the same answer: 'One dollar an acre.' I was shocked at their response, and I thought they were joking, but they assured me they did not need the money, and to be honest, I don't either.

"Both told me that I could not make a better investment. After they returned to their homes, I got to thinking about it and came to the conclusion that the girls are right. My dream to have the family living here is not going to happen. But I can help make Pastor Isaias's dream come true. And when I'm gone and the family returns to visit with friends, that church will mean more to them than anything else I could leave behind."

"I commend you for what you are doing, Will. I don't think you will ever regret your decision. Have you told your daughters of your decision?"

"Not yet, and I'm not sure I want them to know about it right now. I am not looking for any publicity. I've asked the pastor to just say the land was purchased from me and not publicly give a dollar amount."

"I think that is a wise decision. Pastor Isaias already has a contractor drawing up the plans, and now that you have provided a place to build on, this church could very well be built by early June. It would be a wonderful surprise if your daughters and their families were to be present for the first service."

"We'll see. My daughters and their families attended services at Pastor Isaias's church Sunday and really enjoyed it."

"I can't remember their names, but I met your family Sunday. I shook hands with them before they left the service. Small world, huh, Will?"

"They told me an older gentleman about your age had welcomed them along with the pastor and others. But they could not remember your name, and if they had, I would not have recognized it anyway. You are right, Jack, the world does seem to get smaller as we grow older."

Jack thanked Will for his time and invited him to come to the early worship service on Sunday.

Will didn't say he would, but he didn't say he wouldn't.

As Jack drove to the library he remembered that train ride to Texas. It was his first train ride and the first time he had ever been farther from home than a neighboring state. He left as a prodigal son, returned home, and for the first time in his life knew within his heart that, even without Summer, he was in the exact place that God wanted him to be and doing exactly what God wanted him to do.

It was an awesome feeling!

CHAPTER 25

JEREMIAH TELLS ANOTHER STORY

At the library, Jack found a dictionary and looked up that word which defines the study of old coins: numismatics. He was amused to discover that the word numbskull was only a couple of words below numismatics. *This word pretty much describes how I feel when it comes to knowing the value of old coins* he thought.

He typed the word into the search engine on one of the computers in the library and in just a few seconds up popped a list of books on the subject. For the next three hours, Jack pored over every book the library had about coins. His knowledge of numismatics moved from ground zero to about two on a scale of one to ten.

Looks like I've probably let a million bucks slip through my fingers over the years, Jack said to himself. *The old saying that ignorance is bliss is true in my case.*

From time to time he had read in newspapers where someone had found a coin that was worth a fortune. He did not bring the coins he had found at Christ's Church so he could not compare them with the photos of the ones he saw in the books, some of which were worth more than half a million dollars if they were in mint condition and a whole lot less if they had lost their newness.

By the time the librarian tapped him on the shoulder to let him know they closed at 4 p.m. on Saturday, Jack was wishing he had handed this project off to Lamont.

Seeing Jack looking over books on numismatics, she asked if he was a coin collector. He chuckled at the thought and said, "No, but I'd like to know someone who is."

"There's a group of coin collectors in Winston," she advised, "and I think they meet once a month."

"Do you know anyone by name that I may contact?"

"I don't but I think my husband does."

She flipped open her cell phone, hit a couple of buttons and almost instantly her husband answered. Upon her inquiry, he immediately gave her the name and phone number of a member of the group.

Why didn't I talk to the librarian first? Jack thought to himself. *Then again, maybe I've learned just enough to keep people from thinking I'm a numbskull.*

The librarian was kind enough to call Jamie Harper, but there was no answer. Jack wrote down her name and number and thanked the librarian for being so helpful. It wasn't until she walked him to the door that Jack realized he was the last one to leave.

Jack had not had anything to eat since breakfast and his stomach was letting him know it. Instead of going home, he drove to Pastor Isaias's home. If they had no plans, he would take the pastor and Hannah to the Dodge City Steakhouse for supper. They were glad to see Jack and took him up on his offer. On their way out the door, Elder Jeremiah pulled up in the driveway. He gladly accepted the invitation to join them.

During the course of the evening the four got to know each other a little better and found that they had a great deal in common. They laughed at each other's jokes, shared life experiences—both good and bad—and were thankful that in spite of all their struggles, life was still good.

Jack saw things in Hannah and Melanie that made each more special to him. *Hannah does not have the looks that her sister*

Melanie has, he thought, *but she's filled to overflowing with graces within that many beauty queens lack.* Jack simply enjoyed listening to her talk because each word came from the heart. She had no remorse for the past and no animosity toward anyone. Her smile and good sense of humor were unforgettable. The man who had used and abused her before running off with someone else had, in Jack's opinion, left a real jewel. And like a valuable coin that has slipped through one's fingers, he didn't think Hannah's husband would get her back.

Jeremiah, still a bachelor at age fifty, said he was raised in Winston. "What little I know about life on the farm came from stories my parents told me. I never worked in tobacco fields, chopped grass and weeds from a row of peanuts, or shucked an ear of corn. After high school I went to college and earned a degree in accounting. When I returned home I secured a job with the city."

"And Jeremiah has been a valuable member of our church and a dear friend," Pastor Isaias interrupted. He's also a gifted storyteller. Do you have another funny one you can tell us, Jeremiah?"

"I didn't know I had told any funny stories," Jeremiah replied.

"I thought the story about the suitcase was quite funny," said the preacher.

"My daddy didn't think it was funny. He said the only good thing that he got out of his experiences in that section of the county was his wife. Everything else that happened to him was bad."

"What else bad happened to him?" said Pastor Isaias.

"Oscar Williams and my dad could not have been closer had they been twin brothers," Jeremiah began. "If you saw one and not the other, you knew one was nearby, just out of sight. They did everything together. Mr. Dover, Dad's father-in-law, owned some wooded land just off West Gate Road, not too far from where they had found that infamous suitcase.

"This happened in the late 1940s. Animal furs were in big demand. A coon hide would sell for five dollars and you could eat the coon. So when the hunting season came in, my dad and Oscar decided to go hunting for raccoons. They didn't have a dog, but they had a friend who gladly loaned them his.

"Someone told them you wouldn't find any coons if the moon was out. So they picked a dark night when it was not too cold. They parked the car at the end of a path just off West Gate Road. They had done this many times when they had hunted for deer and squirrels, and they were quite familiar with the land. But they had never hunted at night.

"They took the dog into the woods and turned her loose. The owner said she didn't need any instructions on what to do. And old Tootsie, a mixed breed, took off into the dark night. It wasn't long before she began to bark. Thinking she would have that coon up a tree in no time, my dad and Oscar began to follow the dog. After walking for more than an hour through the woods trying to stay up with the dog, they stopped and sat down under an old oak tree to rest. The dog was still barking and chasing something, going one way and then another. Whatever Tootsie was chasing, they no longer believed it was a coon. They tried calling the dog to them, but she would not come.

"They sat under that oak tree until Tootsie's barks consistently came from the same place. And then they went to where she was. She was sitting at the bottom of a sycamore tree, looking up. Using his five-cell flashlight, Oscar began searching the branches of the tree for the coon. He looked first at one side of the tree and then the other. Finally he spotted something. But it wasn't a coon; it was a possum! Possum hides were not in demand, and both men agreed that up to this point in life they had never eaten a possum, and they were not going to start now.

"They had had enough of coon hunting for one night, so they put Tootsie back on her rope and began their trek back to the car. After they had walked for about an hour or so, they realized they had returned to the same sycamore tree they had left. They knew that because that possum was still sitting on that same limb. They had been walking in circles and had to admit they were lost. They were not even sure they were on Mr. Dover's property. It was almost 1 a.m., and they were supposed to be home by midnight.

"They asked themselves, *what do you do when you are lost?* They sat down to rest again and to think. While sitting and thinking of what to do next, they heard the faint sound of a train whistle. Hope filled them. They knew where those railroad tracks were located, and they got up and began walking straight toward the sound they had heard. Thirty minutes later they came to a field with an old barn near where they had exited the woods. Now they knew where they were, two miles from their car.

"Exhausted, the two began the last leg of their journey. My dad and Oscar agreed that they would not tell anyone they had gotten lost. They were going to carry this adventure with them to their graves.

"But they would not have to tell anyone. When they got within a couple hundred yards of their car, they saw lights flashing all around their vehicle and the woods nearby. As they got closer, they realized it was the county sheriff.

"When Dad and Oscar had not returned at the appointed time, their wives had called the sheriff and reported them missing.

"In spite of their efforts to convince the sheriff and friends that they did not get lost, their coon hunting story was the talk of the county after it was published on the front page of *The Gazette.*

"My dad said he and Oscar got more recognition from that night's coon hunt than they would have had they run for sheriff."

Jack just couldn't stop laughing. "I'm sorry, Jeremiah, but that is the funniest story I have heard in a while and I'm looking forward to hearing others." The pastor and Hannah were laughing, too.

Pastor Isaias did not offer up anything about himself until asked about his life in the ministry. He told of the different places he had served and that he had returned to Winston because of his mother's pleas. "It's been a life of ups and downs, walking through valleys and on mountain tops. I've made people happy and I've disappointed others. I've been hurt by people I thought were my best friends and helped by those I thought were my enemies. In all of my trials and tribulations I have tried to be faithful to God, regardless of what that meant to my family, friends, and congregation. God has guided me through the hard times and blessed me in so many ways. I can honestly say that if I had my life to live over again, I would do the same thing."

Smiling at Hannah, he concluded: "One of my greatest blessings is sitting across the table from me tonight."

Hannah seemed embarrassed by the sudden attention, but she had given up her job in a local factory to care for her ailing mother. After her mother died, she stayed home to comfort and care for her dad.

J.R. Sampson, the restaurant owner, came by to see if they had enjoyed their meal and if the service was satisfactory. All expressed their pleasure at both. Jack introduced his guests to J.R. The pastor said he was glad to finally meet one of the most successful men in the county and congratulated him on having a place where families could come together. He invited J.R. and his family to come to worship with them one Sunday, making sure to inform him of the service schedule.

As Jack returned his guests to their home, all agreed they would have to do this again. It had been a wonderful evening of good food and outstanding fellowship.

And Jack suspected that Jeremiah had more funny stories he would enjoy hearing.

CHAPTER 26

LEARNING THE VALUE
OF RARE COINS

After returning home from church Sunday, Jack called Jamie
Harper. He explained how he came by her name and number.
"I would like for someone to look at some old coins I have and
tell me if they are worth anything," Jack explained.

"I'd be glad to and I'm sure the others in our group would
be as well. When did you want to meet?"

"At your convenience. I'm retired and I can meet anytime
and anywhere."

"Our group will meet Tuesday night. There are five of us,
and we take turns meeting in our homes. We will be meeting in
my home this week, and you are welcome to join us. Bring your
coins and we will give you our opinions as to their value."

Jack made a note of the time of the meeting and her address.
He was thrilled at the thought of receiving advice from others in
the community who knew something about coins. He thanked
her and told her he would be there for Tuesday night's meeting.

In preparation for the meeting, Jack separated the coins
according to their original value: pennies in one envelope, nickels in another, dimes, and so on. On the outside of each envelope he recorded the year the coin was minted and descriptive
information, such as "Indian head" or "Lincoln." If they had a
letter on them, he noted that, too. There were seventeen coins.

Jack was the first to arrive at Jamie Harper's home Tuesday night. While waiting for the others in the group to arrive, Jack got to know Jamie's husband, Ronnie, and their two adorable sons, ages six and four.

After everyone was seated around the Harpers' dining room table and introductions were made, the meeting began. They all laughed when Jack told them he had only seventeen coins for them to look at. In their spare time, they would go to the bank and get rolls of coins and go through them and pick out ones they thought might be of value. And whenever they purchased anything, they would check the coins they received as change. They were full-time treasure hunters.

All wanted to know where Jack obtained the coins and what he planned to do with them.

"I found them beneath the oldest black church in the county," said Jack, "and any money from the sale of the coins will go toward rebuilding Christ's Church in Winston."

Everyone knew about the rebuilding of the church through articles they had read in *The Gazette*.

Their first order of business was to review the coins Jack had brought to the meeting. They looked at all the pennies first, carefully inspecting each individually, and then they put them back in the envelope—except for one. It was a 1914 penny with a head of wheat on the front and the letter D on it. It was worn but not so worn that one could not see the date, the D and the head of wheat. They all agreed this one was worth taking to a dealer for appraisal.

They found two of the nickels worthy of appraisal also: a 1924 D Buffalo nickel and a 1926 S Buffalo nickel.

One dime, a 1927 S Mercury, was deemed worthy of appraisal, and all the remaining coins were thought to be worth little more than their face value.

They would not venture placing a price tag on the coins, emphasizing that the value of rare coins was determined by their condition.

All of the numismatists recommended that Jack either take the coins to a dealer for appraisal or email them photos of the coins and see if they would be interested in buying them. He learned that the nearest dealer was in Rockton, and a couple of others were located in the Capital City.

Jack expressed his appreciation to the group for sharing their expertise and told them he would let them know what the outcome was.

The next morning Jack took his digital camera and snapped photos of both sides of the four coins recommended for appraisal. He then located the web pages of three dealers. Just as he'd been told, the dealers invited sellers to visit their businesses or send them photos by email, and Jack took them up on their latter offer.

He asked the dealers to place a value on each coin and to inform him if they were interested in purchasing them. He included a photo of each coin in a separate attachment and hit send.

CHAPTER 27

PLANTING TREES AND GROWING YOUTH

After sending the photos, Jack was thankful he could take a break from the building project and work on a task he had in mind. Winter was waning and another growing season was about to begin. The time was perfect for planting trees.

Beaver had cut down many of the young cypress trees along the edges of the swamps on his property. And the area between the swamps and the ridges had grown up in scrubby bushes and trees of little value.

"Why are you planting trees that you will not live long enough to sit under for shade?" asked one of Jack's great nephews, who had dropped by for a visit.

"I'm not doing this as an investment for myself," Jack explained. "As owner of the land, I'm responsible for taking care of it, and to me that means doing the very best I can so that the next owner will reap the most benefits possible. That someone else will benefit from my labors brings me joy. I reaped the rewards of my father's work. And I expect my children to reap the rewards of my labors. I want them to say I did an excellent job.

"Dad told me we are inspired not by what others say but by what they do. I hope that what I'm doing is an inspiration to you and others who might be thinking as you are."

Jack's plan was to plant one hundred cypress trees in or near the swamps and one hundred white oak trees in the area between the swamps and the ridges, where they would grow best. He had ordered the trees from the state forestry service near Gold City a few days earlier. Rather than have them shipped, he chose to pick them up.

On his way to Gold City to procure the trees, Jack's memory bank overflowed with thoughts of the good times he once had there with his late wife, family, and friends. He also thought about his relationship with Summer Brown. She was still on his mind, even though she had not responded to any of his phone calls, cards, or letters. His first stop in Gold City would be her home.

Jack was nervous when he pulled into Summer's driveway. Her car was in the garage, but that was not a sure sign that she would be home. Except for a dog barking in the distance, it was quiet. He took a deep breath and rang the doorbell. He heard no sounds coming from inside, except for the doorbell ringing. He waited for a moment before pushing the button again, three times in succession. There was no answer. Then he knocked on the door. If she were home, she was not coming to the door.

Disappointed, Jack wrote a note to say he had stopped by and to tell her he still loved her. He placed the note inside the storm door.

As he returned to his truck, Jack saw that the flowerbed that once bloomed like their relationship was now a bed of weeds. And he wondered if he had become just another weed in her garden of life.

Jack took the long way to the nursery so he could stop by the church he and Summer once attended. Pastor Tom Gregory was glad to see him. "I hope you are coming back to Gold City," he said with a smile.

"I miss your lively sermons and the fellowship, Pastor Tom, but God has put me to work in Cobbwebb County."

"What brings you back to Gold City, then?"

Jack informed him of his mission and his desire to see Summer again. "I stopped to see you and to find out if you know how Summer is doing."

"I'm afraid I can't be of much help. When you left, she pretty much quit coming to church. We have been unsuccessful in ministering to her because we have been unable to contact her. I heard that she has spent some time visiting with her family in Pennsylvania and a daughter in Tennessee. I've only seen her a couple of times since the two of you sat together in church."

"Was she alone or with someone?"

"She was alone on both occasions."

"I have not seen or communicated with her since I left Gold City, though I have tried many times. If you see her again, please tell her that I came by and asked about her. I'd love to see her again."

"I'm sorry things didn't work out the way you hoped they would, Jack. I sense that your affection for her has not changed. I'll speak to some of the people she used to be friends with and see if they know more than I do. I'll let you know if I find out anything to put your mind at ease."

Jack gave the pastor his phone number and address and expressed his gratitude for his support and concern.

With a heavy heart, Jack picked up the saplings. As he drove back to Winston he had a strange feeling that not all was well with Summer. He prayed he was wrong and still held on to the hope that one day they could at least be friends again, if not soul mates.

Jack worked from sunup to sundown the remainder of the week putting the saplings in the ground. It was good therapy.

By the end of the day Friday he had freed himself of the sadness that had come over him and he was pleased with what he had done. He was glad the week was over, too, because his old body was sore and aching.

When he returned home after planting the last cypress tree, there were two messages on his answering machine, one from his brother inviting him to have supper with the family and the other from Zinnia, the reporter for *The Gazette.*

It was too late to call Zinnia, but he suspected his brother's wife was either cooking supper or had it on the table. He took a quick shower and drove to his brother's house, knowing that even if he were late there would be plenty of food. Mark and Sammie—and enough children and grandchildren to fill the seats around the table—were enjoying another of Sammie's sumptuous meals: collards, rutabagas, black-eyed peas, boiled potatoes, butterbeans and corn, cornbread and biscuits, fried chicken, baked ham, sweet potatoes, and candied yams. There was so much food that it would not all fit the table; some was still on the stove. For desserts there were a multi-tiered chocolate cake and sweet potato pie sitting on another counter. Jack ate small portions to try to hide his empty stomach, but went back several times for more. He believed that Sammie was the last of the great cooks in Cobbwebb County and was pretty sure that neither he nor anyone else in the family would get another meal like Sammie's when she was no longer able to prepare them.

Jack helped Sammie clean up after the meal and spent an hour conversing with great nephews and nieces. Some were still in college and some were married and employed. They all wanted to know why Jack was working with the black community to rebuild Christ's Church, and they wanted to know why Jack was worshipping with a black church.

Jack's relatives, like he had when he was young, had passed black churches to get to a white church. Although he knew the answer, Jack asked, "Have you ever attended a church that was predominantly black?"

Their responses were all the same, "No."

"Why not?" he said. "Blacks and whites go to the same schools, same restaurants, work side-by-side, sleep in the same hotels and motels, shop in the same stores, are treated by the same doctors, go to the same hospitals, same retirement homes, worship the same God, but don't go to church together."

Their answers varied, but none offered a valid reason for never having worshipped in a predominantly black church.

Jack wondered what kind of answers he would receive if he asked the same question to a group of young black people about why they had never worshipped in a predominantly white church.

"Let me explain why I am going to a church that is made up mostly of black people," Jack began. "I made a commitment to God that when I came back here I would reach out to the people I had once rejected. At least in this area of my life I was going to start over and try to do a better job.

"The first time I attended The Ark of Salvation Church in Winston, I was the only white person in the congregation. But I felt comfortable. Pastor Isaias is a good and honorable man, humble, quiet, but committed to fulfilling his duties as a pastor and his promise to his mother that he would rebuild Christ's Church. He not only knows and preaches the Word, but also lives it. His sermons are uplifting, and you get the feeling that he has a spirit of hope that we can work together and make our community better. I consider him, his two daughters, and his grandson friends. They are wonderful people. I wonder how many others like them I failed to get to know for the same reasons you have given me tonight about why you have never been to a black church. I feel that I have missed out on many blessings because I have looked at the world as being divided into black and white when it comes to the church.

"Blacks should go to white churches occasionally and whites to black churches," he added. "I think it would do all of us good, and it would help destroy the myth that black and white churches are so different that blacks and whites can't come together and worship God.

"I hope I'm not preaching," he laughed. "And I hope I have answered your question. Libby is going to attend the 8:30 service with me Sunday. This will be her first time worshipping in a black church. I hope you will join us."

No one made a commitment to join Jack, but they didn't say they wouldn't attend.

Jack gave his heartfelt thanks to Mark and Sammie for another wonderful meal and a chance to fellowship with the family. He said good night and before departing reminded his nieces and nephews that experience is the greatest teacher.

CHAPTER 28

WHAT YOU CAN'T SEE FROM
THE HIGHWAY

Sunday morning, Jack picked up his niece Libby on the way to church. They arrived early. As he looked around, he was pleased to see a good number of people he knew. There were Zinnia Gregory, Zeb Johnson and his wife, Lamont and his mother Melanie Epstein, and A.J. Tinsley. He did not see any of his brother's family but he didn't lose heart. Jack and Libby sat in the pew directly behind Zinnia, who asked to speak with Jack after the service.

Just before the service began, two of Mark's grandsons and their mother entered and found their way to Jack and Libby's pew. Jack and Libby were all smiles as they welcomed them. The Ark of Salvation Church was conducting two worship services, and Jack was surprised to see that most of the seats were filled for the first service.

The congregational singing was uplifting. Prayers were made for the sick and for the work of the church and its leaders. Pastor Isaias announced that three acres of land had been purchased from a benevolent member of the community for an unbelievable price. That brought a big round of applause and shouts of *Amen* and *Halleluiah* from the congregation. It was also announced that a representative from East Coast Builders, Inc. would be giving a presentation Wednesday night on a proposed building for Christ's Church. That elicited another round of applause and shouts of praise. With much gusto, the choir sang, "Do Lord Remember Me."

Pastor Isaias's sermon for the morning was taken from Luke chapter 15, which told the story of Jesus healing a leper by touching him. There was silence in the congregation as the pastor explained how God's chosen people looked at those with leprosy. "They were outcasts, isolated from anyone except others with leprosy, forced to live outside the city walls, not permitted to touch another human—their very lives dependent upon relatives and the mercy of others.

"Jesus, the Son of God, reached out His hand and touched this man and healed him. When the greatest gets together with the lowest, miracles happen," he proclaimed. "In the eyes of God, we are all like the leper; we are unclean and unholy, and we cannot be healed unless we are cleansed by the blood of Jesus."

To close out the service, Pastor Isaias asked anyone who wanted to be touched by Jesus to come to the altar and receive prayer. Jack did not know why, but he was the first to walk down the aisle. And before he knew it, most members of the congregation were standing up front with him. As the pastor prayed, the choir sang "Peace in the Valley." Most in attendance said it was a mountain top experience, a service in which all the right things were said and all the right songs sung, and people left the service knowing they had been touched in a way they could not explain.

Outside, Jack's niece and great-nephews were amazed at what they had experienced and vowed that they would come again.

Jack waited until Zinnia came out. She wanted to know when she could come for the interview. Jack promised to check the weather and call her Monday morning with a day and time.

After reviewing the weather forecast, Jack chose Wednesday and promptly called Zinnia. She agreed to meet him at 10 a.m. Before hanging up, she said, "And remember, I'll be asking the questions this time!"

That put a smile on Jack's face.

Before the sun came up Wednesday, Jack had fixed himself a hearty breakfast of eggs, pancakes, and sausage. He put a meal in the crockpot consisting of pork chops, potatoes, carrots, and onions. He knew he'd want something to eat when he and Zinnia completed their tour of the swamps.

It was a perfect day, and Jack thanked Mother Nature for not making a liar out of the weather forecaster.

Zinnia grabbed her tape recorder and camera and her jacket. Except for a hat, she was well dressed for the occasion. Jack loaned her a pink hat his wife used to wear. They climbed into Jack's pickup truck and headed to the old boat landing at the north end of the farm.

"I'm glad you asked me to show you the swamps, Zinnia. People cannot say they have seen a swamp when they zip past them at fifty-five miles per hour on a four-lane highway."

Jack put on his life jacket and helped Zinnia into hers. They boarded Jack's flat-bottom boat. He asked her to turn off her cell phone so they could hear the natural sounds in the forest, and she complied.

"Have you ever been on a boat, Zinnia?"

"No. I've never had the opportunity until now."

"You're not scared are you?"

"I'm apprehensive, but not scared."

Jack had her sit in the front of the boat facing him. He wanted to see the expression on her face as they weaved their way through the mass of trees to the Poopah River.

With the trolling motor, they quietly glided through the water unnoticed. Halfway to the Poopah River, Jack stopped in the middle of the huge swamp. They sat in the boat and listened to the sounds of nature. They saw some ducks fly in and land on the water. An egret flew over their boat. They listened to the birds chirping. Something splashed in the water some distance away, and Jack suspected it was a beaver.

Zinnia had seen cypress trees from the road and just saw them as trees. Observing them from the swamp, rising majestically toward the blue sky, was exhilarating to her. Now she could tell this tree was different from all other trees. As he watched Zinnia, Jack could only imagine what she was thinking. He suspected he was observing what he had himself always observed, that, like people, from a distance all trees look about the same, but seeing them up close and personal, they are all different. Jack could see her wonder in entering a strange place fade away, overcome by the peace and quiet of the swamp. She did not say a word, just looked up and around and drank in the beauty and tranquility this place offered.

"I cannot remember being anywhere this quiet," Zinnia said. "It is so quiet that you notice it. It makes you realize how noisy our world is."

Jack let her turn her back to him as they moved on through the swamp so that she could see what he was seeing. Now she understood what she could not have known standing on the shore: in this mass of trees was a road, almost like a canal carved out in the swamp.

As they passed a pine ridge, Zinnia asked if Native Americans ever lived there.

"They did, although I don't know what tribe they belonged to. I know they lived on this pine ridge because I have found shards of pottery and many arrowheads there."

Zinnia remained quiet and observant until they exited the swamp and entered the Poopah River.

"Is this the river that runs past Winston?" she asked.

"Yes."

"It smells different; it's like entering another world."

Jack motored up the river and once again entered the swamps through Moccasin Ditch. Moss was hanging everywhere in the trees. Zinnia looked up into the forest canopy and saw the moss with the sun shining through it as it swayed in a breeze.

"What are those things sticking out of the water?" she asked.

"Cypress knees. They are part of the support system."

"You can't see these from the road. They remind me of spires that rise from cathedrals," she said. "What kind of trees are those with the big bottoms?"

"Tupelo gums."

"Why don't they have knees to hold them up?"

"They are not needed. Their huge foundation and deep roots are sufficient to keep them upright."

As they made their way back to the boat landing, they saw two deer standing at the edge of the swamp looking at them. Zinnia got a picture of them before they were spooked and ran up onto the ridge. And before she and Jack returned to the place where they started, she also took photos of a flock of turkeys feeding on one of the ridges.

As Jack guided the boat onto the spot from where they had departed, they heard a strange sound.

"What was that?"

"That was a wise old owl welcoming us back to the farm," Jack answered with a big grin on his face.

Before getting out of the boat, Zinnia turned to look at the swamp once more. As Jack observed her contemplating what she had just experienced, he was reminded of a time long ago. As he was thinking about his youth, Zinnia interrupted his thoughts. "Why are you staring at me like that, Jack?"

"I'm sorry, Zinnia, I didn't realize I was staring at you. Something in my past just popped up unexpectedly, and I did not mean to make you uncomfortable. While my eyes may have been focused on you, I was looking beyond you to the time when I was growing up."

"I don't understand what you are getting at," she said.

"In my youth, Zinnia, there was an unwritten code of conduct which said that I was not to touch a black girl, simply because she was black. It took me a long time to see the error of this way of looking at people who are different.

"You remind me of some of the pretty young black girls I used to know from a distance. We could work together in the fields and we'd see each other from time to time when I walked passed their homes or saw them in town, but I never really got to know them because I was not supposed to cross the color line.

"If I could return to my youth with my newfound knowledge, I would get to know them on a personal basis. God has forgiven me of my transgressions, but I have not forgotten them.

"I hope I have not embarrassed you by telling you this, but I can't help but look at my life and see how I have robbed myself of meeting and enjoying the company of others like you and Pastor Isaias because of my skewed way of seeing the world."

"I must say I am a bit surprised that you would share such personal thoughts with me, Jack. I know from experience there are others who still look at the world as you did when you were young, but they are a minority.

"I will not include your confession in my story, but I will not forget what you have shared with me. Without realizing it, you have made me feel good about myself and proud of who I am, and for that I am grateful."

As they traveled from the north end of the farm to Jack's house, Zinnia was in awe at the size of the farm. The farm was more visible on the way back because of its shape.

"And your family tilled all this land with mules and horses?" she asked.

"We had several families living on the farms, and most of them were family members."

As they came upon the last remaining tenant farmhouse, Zinnia asked if she could go inside. Jack gladly agreed to show her a home very similar to the one in which he was raised. This particular old home was now used for storage.

Inside the front door were the living room and a portioned-off bedroom. Signs of a wood stove were visible in the corner. In the back of the house was the dining and kitchen area, where food was prepared on a stove powered with wood. The building had no insulation or electricity. The one-story home had a tin roof.

"I'll appreciate my apartment much more now that I've seen what people used to live in. Did black people live here?"

"No. All the tenant farmers who lived on my dad's farms were white, but there was little difference between the homes of black and white tenant farmers."

It was 1:30 when they returned to Jack's house. He heated a can of garden peas in the microwave to go with the crock-pot meal he'd prepared earlier. They had sweet iced tea with their meal. Both were hungry and the food tasted much better than it would have if they hadn't been.

While eating their lunch, Zinnia asked Jack a few more questions about growing up in this isolated part of the county and how they managed to survive the depression without any support from the government.

She also wanted to know how blacks and whites got along together.

"Even though we did not socialize, we got along well. We worked together in the fields, and I remember my dad giving food from our smokehouse to the ones who came and asked. I also saw him lend money to blacks and whites that he knew would never repay him. There were no locks on our barns or homes, and we never had a problem with anyone stealing from us. Dad knew the blacks hunted on his property, but he never said anything to them about it. Life was hard back then, even harder for blacks, and I think dad realized that, so he did what he could to help them. Until I discovered the logbook at Christ's Church, I did not know my dad had helped to build the church."

By now it was apparent that Zinnia would not return to Winston on time, so Jack advised her to tell Zeb that her tardiness was his fault. She thanked Jack for all the trouble he had gone through to make this an eventful day for her.

"You've given me more than a great story. You've given me some memories that will last for a lifetime. I will always be indebted to you for your kindness."

Jack had enjoyed the day, too. And knowing that he had made it special for someone he admired and was fond of made it even more enjoyable and special to him.

CHAPTER 29

SWAMPS AND SWAMP PEOPLE

The story Zinnia Gregory wrote about Jack Porter appeared in Thursday's *Gazette*. Jack was confident he knew what she would say about him, but he was anxious to learn what she had to say about the swamps, so he made a special trip to Winston to procure a copy of the paper fresh off the press. Zinnia was out on assignment, but Zeb Johnson was in, and he gladly gave Jack a copy of *The Gazette*.

"Must be something mighty important in this issue for you to drive all the way to town just to get a copy when one will be delivered to you on Friday morning," Zeb commented. "Would it be the story she did on you?"

"No," said Jack. "I want to see what she has to say about our swamps."

"I think you will be surprised at what she wrote," said Zeb.

Jack thanked Zeb for the paper and returned to his pickup. The story began on page 1 and jumped to page 3 where the sidebar on the swamp excursion was highlighted in a box with a wavy black border.

Jack leaned back in the seat of his pickup and began reading.

In the two plus years I have lived in Cobbwebb County I have heard comments from many people about the swamps and those who live or grew up in the swamps. Most of the comments were negative. I was given the impression that somehow these swamps and swamp people are not on par with the rest of the county.

Jack Porter grew up in the swamps along the Polongo River. He left home at the age of eighteen and did not return until forty years later. During that time he lived on three different continents, in half a dozen states, and traveled through most of the other states. He has seen most of the free world, and yet, when it came time for him to choose a place to spend the remaining years of his life, he returned to the swamps where he was raised.

I have seen the mountains and I have enjoyed the beaches on the East Coast, I have been to big cities and small towns, but not until yesterday had I ever been in a swamp, even though I have driven past hundreds of them. At my request, Jack Porter took me into some of the swamps he came to love as a youth.

You have not seen the truly beautiful part of this county until you have been in one of its swamps, where cypress and tupelo gum trees reach for the stars. There are roads in the swamps, for those who know where to look, that make the swamps as easy to navigate as our highway system. If anything in America still resembles what the nation looked like when Columbus discovered the continent, it is the swamps. Though there is some pollution and debris that has floated downriver and into the swamps, there are no dumps, subdivisions, slums, businesses, or paved roads. During our two-hour journey into the swamps to the Poopah River and back to where we began, we did not see another person. I can't remember ever going anywhere and not seeing another soul.

It was not until Jack cut off the trolling motor and we stopped in the middle of the swamp did I realize how noisy our world is. I thought about the noise in the office where I work as I sat in the boat. The printing press would have been running, phones ringing, people talking all around me, and traffic going and coming on the street outside. But in the swamp there were only natural sounds. It is the quietest and most peaceful place I have ever been.

I saw moss hanging in the trees and gently swaying in the cool breeze. It reminded me of a Walt Disney movie. I saw cypress knees on the banks of Moccasin Ditch that reminded me of cathedrals. I heard natural sounds in the swamps that I have never heard before and that cannot be found anywhere else. Though Jack said at times the swamp gave off an odor, on this occasion it smelled clean and fresh, and breathing the air was exhilarating. Looking up into the blue sky, the canopy of trees covered us like umbrellas. I saw a flock of wild turkeys and deer in their habitat. I saw a beaver lodge for the first time, and Jack showed me a ridge where Native Americans once lived near the Poopah River.

The eyes of this city girl were opened to a new world, a world without rush hour traffic, brick and mortar, or flashing lights—a world almost free of the noise humans create around the clock.

If I had to describe my first journey into the swamps in just one word, it is "unforgettable."

And if other swamp people are anything like Jack Porter, they are my kind of people.

Now I know why Jack returned to his roots.

Brilliant. A brilliant piece of writing, Jack thought to himself. He was awed at the way she had attacked the stereotyping of people who live in a different environment. It never bothered him that people called him a swamp rat, but after reading her article he had to admit that he felt really good about himself and the place he had chosen to spend the rest of his life.

CHAPTER 30

CHRIST'S CHURCH APPEARS ON THE RADAR SCREEN

Jack returned home and checked his e-mail. He had received one from a coin dealer in the Capital City and one from Rockton.

Both responses were encouraging. While they did not give any guarantees, both dealers estimated that the four coins could bring between $5,000 and $6,000. They offered to take the coins and place them in markets where coin dealers throughout the country could view them through their websites and take five percent of the sale price for their efforts when sold. That sounded like a fair deal to Jack, but he didn't want to do anything until he coordinated it with Pastor Isaias.

Two representatives from East Coast Builders, Inc. arrived in Winston Wednesday afternoon. Brooks Allen was the chief architect for the company and Alonso Decker was the company's cost analyst.

Pastor Isaias met them at the church and took them to the building site. They would have to figure into their cost both site preparation for the building and parking space. After viewing the site, they returned to the church and set up their equipment for their 6 p.m. presentation to the congregation. Jeremiah took them to a restaurant on the Poopah River where they could dine and relax before the presentation.

The meeting began shortly after six, and most of the seats in the sanctuary were filled with members and others interested in seeing the church built. The pastor expressed his appreciation for the good attendance and welcomed everyone to the meeting. After praying for the success of the building project, he turned the meeting over to Brooks and Alonso.

Brooks was the first to speak, and he commended the congregation for the site they had selected for the building. Knowing that most churches do not have all the money needed to build a first-class facility, he presented three plans: first class, middle of the road, and essentials only.

He showed an artist's conception of what the church would look like from the outside regardless of which plan was selected. He presented the most expensive version first, and then pointed out how the church could reduce costs by selecting one of the other plans. After their presentation, Brooks and Alonso answered a multitude of questions. The price tag for the three plans: $110,000, $100,000, and $95,000. The cost analyst provided an estimated cost on things which could be done later either by a contractor or volunteer laborers. For example, church members could paint the facility, and the parking lot could be paved later. The baptistery could also be installed later.

Copies of the three plans and estimated costs were left with the congregation. Once the church decided exactly what they wanted the contractor to do, a contract would be written and signed. Work could begin immediately after the signing of the contract. If construction began in February, and the weather cooperated, the building would be ready for worship in June.

Pastor Isaias expressed his appreciation to Brooks and Alonso and told them the leaders of the church would get together and decide what they wanted and get back to them. He closed the meeting with prayer.

The resurrection of Christ's Church was finally on the radar screen. The hard part was about to begin. Enough money was available to get started, and the pastor was sure the bank would lend them whatever they needed to finish the job. But they had to decide on which plan they wanted to go with.

After the meeting, Jack met with Pastor Isaias and Jeremiah and updated them on the coins found in the old church building. "I'm surprised at the value of the coins," said Pastor Isaias. "Let's go with the dealer in Rockton.

"I'd like to have you sit in on the meeting, Jack, with church leaders when we discuss how much money we want to put into the church building."

"Thanks for asking. I'd love to. Just let me know when."

The next day Jack decided to take the coins to Rockton, but he didn't want to go alone, so he called Hannah. "Do you think you could talk your dad into letting me take you out for lunch today?" asked Jack jokingly.

"I ain't asking, Jack. What time are you picking me up?"

One of the many things Jack loved about Hannah was her sense of humor. She had not let circumstances destroy the kid in her.

They left Winston at ten thirty and arrived at the coin dealer's office in Rockton an hour later. By noon they had turned the coins over to the dealer with instructions to mail the check from any sales to Pastor Isaias and provided a stamped self-addressed envelope.

Jack had planned to take Hannah to a good seafood restaurant, but Hannah asked to go to a cafeteria where she could find food that would be better for her diet.

The coin dealer suggested they go to Andy's Cafeteria, a privately owned restaurant that specialized in serving locally grown vegetables and health foods especially for people who were on diets. They entered the business shortly after noon, and though it was quite busy, they found a booth in the corner where they could dine and carry on a conversation with some privacy.

After their meal was served, Jack said the blessing and thanked God that he had a friend like Hannah to share part of his life with.

Hannah smiled at Jack and thanked him for his kind words. "If I had said the blessing I would have said the same thing about you.

"I want you to know, Jack, that you are the first white man who has ever taken me, all by myself, out to dinner. That might not mean anything to you, but it means the world to me. I can't thank you enough because I know that you are doing it for the right reason."

Jack was touched by her remarks. It had never occurred to him that such a simple gesture of friendship could mean so much to her.

"I wanted to do something for you, Hannah, to express my appreciation for all that you have done for me personally and for the church fundraising project. You have been a blessing to me and a joy to work with. And I don't feel that this dinner is nearly enough for what you have done."

"It is for me, Jack. My marriage was not a good one, and I have put that in the past. I have not gotten a divorce because I have neither wanted nor pursued another relationship of any kind. And I know that you are not courting me, but you can't understand how much it means to me to sit across the table from a white man who looks at me, not as a black woman, but as a friend that he loves to fellowship with. There are a lot of women like me who are just looking for companionship and appreciation, and you have given me both."

Jack simultaneously felt like crying and kicking himself in the rear end for not doing this sooner.

"Thanks for sharing a part of your heart with me, Hannah. I have to admit that I had no idea how much this would mean to you, and now that I know, I promise that we will do this more often because I do enjoy spending time with you."

"I have not seen you with another woman, but I suspect that there is a reason for it."

"There is one in my heart, Hannah, but I don't know if she will ever be a part of my life. I try not to think about her, and I am beginning to lose hope. I trust that God will do what is best for both of us.

"When I returned to Cobbwebb County, I vowed that with God's help I would change some things in my life that I believed needed changing. I can preach only one sermon to the world, and that is through the way I live my life. There were times when people did not get a good sermon because my life was not what it should have been. When I leave this world, I do not want anyone to say that this last part of my sermon was not in sync with the Good Book that I read and try to follow every day."

"I haven't met anyone who is perfect, Jack, but you and my dad come as close as anyone I know."

"Thank you for telling me that. I'm not a saint, but I try my best to live ever day what I believe. And for you to say that means I must be walking down the right road.

"I hope you don't mind me asking, but are you trying to lose weight or are you dieting for medical reasons?"

"I'm trying to lose weight. If I had the money I'd join the Y. I go for walks when I can, but I don't like to go alone. We live in a world that has too many evil people in it."

"Yes, we do," Jack agreed. "Maybe we can go for walks together on Saturdays, weather permitting."

"I'd love that."

The last time Jack had enjoyed being with a woman this much was when he and Summer were dating.

It was after one thirty when they left the restaurant. After dropping Hannah off around three, Jack went to the Family Y in Winston. He purchased her a full membership for one year and asked the lady to mail the membership card to her as a gift from a friend.

When Jack returned home, he had a message from Pastor Isaias on his answering machine. The big meeting was scheduled that night at six at the church. He called the pastor to let him know he had gotten his message and that he would be there.

Jack arrived a few minutes before six and followed others who were going into the meeting room. They all looked at Jack, perhaps wondering why he was there. Pastor Isaias was the last to arrive. Five men and one woman were present, besides Jack, the pastor, and Jeremiah.

After introducing Jack, the pastor explained to the leaders that he had asked him to sit in on the meeting and listen to what board members had to say about the direction of the building project. "When we are through, I am going to ask Jack for his input.

"Jack is not a member of our church," he added, "but he is well aware of our situation and since he has played a large part in helping us raise funds for the new building, I thought it would be wise to have him here tonight. I trust him completely and respect his opinions."

With that said, the meeting began with prayer, after which Pastor Isaias asked Jeremiah for an update on the money collected for Christ's Church. Since Jeremiah was the treasurer for The Ark of Salvation Church, he had agreed to keep the records for Christ's Church as well.

"I don't have the exact figure," Jeremiah reported, "but it is almost $70,000."

They were all amazed at the amount of money that had been raised through the sale of the old building and the land and contributions, not to mention the donation of three acres of land.

"Add the value of the land to the $70,000 and we have $90,000 in assets," Jeremiah advised.

Pastor Isaias took a vote to see who wanted to go with the turn-key package. Only Jeremiah voted for it. He asked how many wanted to go with the middle-of-the-road plan. Only one voted for it.

"I assume the rest want to go with the essentials-only version," the pastor stated.

And the responses were a unanimous "yea" from the rest of the group.

Over the course of the next hour, Jack listened as the church leaders discussed the building project. The *can nots* were in control. "It is not the time to be borrowing more money." "We don't have anyone who can do much of the work." "We are going to need another preacher." "We shouldn't put another burden on our members." "If we fail, the community will laugh at us."

They kept on about what they couldn't do, until finally, the pastor brought the discussion to an end and asked Jack to give his input.

As Jack stood up to go to the front of the room, he thought to himself, *These people have been given $70,000 plus land to build on and still they cannot see the blessings that God is pouring out on them. How can I persuade them,* he wondered, *that God will give them everything they need if they will only believe?*

Jack thanked Pastor Isaias for his faith in him and looked at the group gathered before him. He paused briefly to put his thoughts in order.

"Five of you voted to build a church with the bare necessities," Jack began. "One voted for the middle of the road, and one for the turn-key facility. If I could vote, I would side with Jeremiah.

"The most expensive of the plans presented to the congregation is not for a cathedral or a magnificent piece of architecture. It is for an attractive building, structured and designed for God's people to come together to worship Him. There is nothing in the plan that is extravagant, wasteful, or unnecessary.

"I don't know anyone in this county who wants to see this project fail. Everyone is pulling for it and praying for it. When Christ's Church is completed, people are going to want to come by and see what you have done. You do not want to be embarrassed by what they see.

"Over the past few months I have seen God working in my life and in the life of your pastor, and in the lives of many others I know. God has given you $70,000. It's nothing short of a miracle. God is involved in this building project, so it cannot fail.

"Tonight you have come to the fork in the road in the life of this church. You are being given the chance to take the high road or the low road. I beg you to take the high road.

"Make a commitment now that with God's blessings you are going to raise another $40,000 so that Christ's Church will be debt-free when the first worship service is conducted. Then go out tomorrow and tell the world what your plans are and see what happens.

"When I was a college student, my wife gave me a lapel button. Written over the image of a frog were these words: 'You gotta go with what you got.'

"God has given this congregation people with the capabilities needed to build this church. So go with what you've got. When God looks down here, He does not want to see His people wandering in the wilderness of doubt. He wants to see you doing something. Have yard sales. Cut someone's grass and put the money in the Christ's Church bank account. When people see that you are serious about what you are doing, they will give more than is expected of them.

"You are the leaders of this church. I pray that you will stand up and make a decision, not based on what you can do, but what God can do through you."

With that, Jack left the meeting.

CHAPTER 31

THEY TAKE THE HIGH ROAD

Pastor Isaias called Jack around nine that night to let him know they were taking the high road and to thank him for his input.

"I don't know if I could have persuaded them on my own to come to this decision," Pastor Isaias said. "After you left, I told them that I did not know if our ancestors are watching us from heaven. But what I do know is that the eyes of the folks in Cobbwebb County are focused on us. If we embarrass ourselves, I can't believe that we are pleasing God. With the resources we have, I could not think of a single reason why we cannot build a facility that would honor God and make our community proud."

Jack had to say *amen* to that!

The unanimous decision was received with much applause and enthusiasm by the congregation the following Sunday. And things began to happen which reflected their newfound breath of energy.

The choir decided to put a program together and offer to sing at other churches for a love offering that would go toward the building of Christ's Church.

A group got together on Saturdays to have yard sales in the parking lot of a local business. Members of the community could contribute items which would then be sold on their behalf for ten percent of the price, proceeds going to the Christ's Church building fund. The group, made up mostly of teenagers, called themselves The Young Recyclers.

Many of the town's businesses agreed to place a container near their cash registers where customers could contribute if they wished. With each week's report on the progress of raising the additional funds, excitement continued to build.

The twelve-member choir—with a pianist—named itself "The Singing Disciples." Jack learned that Hannah and Melanie had once been a popular duo before graduating from high school and moving on to college and a career. Melanie's skills on the keyboard, though a bit rusty now, were once the talk of the county, and Hannah had a voice that some thought could have made it in the big-time world of music.

He learned that they had quit singing when their mother died. But something within them said it was time to get back on the stage. Although they were just getting started, Jack knew they would only get better.

On Valentine's Day Jack went to the pastry shop on Main Street to have coffee and a sweet roll with some of his relatives he had not seen for a while. He enjoyed staying in touch with his kinfolk, and he felt that a good way to do it was over food.

As they were just biting into their desserts, Zeb Johnson came in for a cup of coffee. He dropped by Jack's table to say hello. "My timing is good today, Jack, because I've been meaning to call and ask you to drop by the office."

"If I'm not in any trouble, I'll be over shortly."

"You're not in any trouble . . . yet!" Zeb chuckled.

On his way to Zeb's office, Jack stopped by the Nutty Chocolate Shop, appropriately named for its main product:

chocolate-covered nuts. It was only midmorning, and the shop was already crowded. Jack found a small but expensive box of chocolates made with pecans. He asked the sales lady to write on the box: *TO: Zinnia; FROM: Your Secret Admirer.*

From there, Jack went to see Zeb. After chatting casually for a few moments, Jack asked Zeb what was on his mind.

"I've been thinking about doing something to help raise money for Christ's Church," said Zeb. "I told the community some time ago that we would stand with the believers who wanted to see this old church resurrected. And I am not one to just stand by and watch it happen. I've got to do something besides write about it."

"What have you got in mind, Zeb?"

"I'm getting feedback that the choir is quite good. They are performing at churches, and as you and I know, there are people who don't go to church who would go somewhere else to hear a good concert."

"Great idea!"

"I need your help with this project," Zeb pleaded. "I know that when you worked at the base near Gold City you were constantly involved in events that brought people together. I'm thinking of a dinner on a Saturday night with the choir as the main attraction. *The Gazette* will be the sponsor and all proceeds will go into the Christ's Church building fund. I'd like to have you head up this project for me."

Jack sat quietly for a moment, considering all the work that would have to go into pulling this off. But he could not refuse Zeb. *If anything of value happens in a community, it needs people like Zeb to make it happen,* he thought.

"I'll do it," Jack said. "I appreciate your confidence and trust in me, and I'll do my best to put together a team of people who will make this an evening to remember. Got any suggestions?"

"None; I am going to let you take it from here. My only thought is that the more people we can get involved, the better. Keep me posted and let me know how I can help you."

Before leaving to come up with a plan, Jack gave Zeb the box of chocolates and asked him to deliver it to Zinnia, with instructions that he was not to tell her it came from him.

The Singing Disciples had decided to perform one concert every week, preferably on Sunday night, until funds were raised to build Christ's Church. They had performed twice, but Jack was unable to attend either of those events, and he was not going to miss the third one. It would be at Crossroads Baptist Church, where he was a member before he enlisted in the Air Force. Libby was still a member there, and the two of them contacted everyone they knew, family and friends, to encourage them to attend.

Crossroads was a small church, seating about 100 people. Libby had never seen a black choir perform there, so she was not sure how many people would show up to hear them. She needn't have worried. People started arriving early, and by six o'clock the place was packed. The choir was in place and ready to perform.

Not since the day he had walked down the aisle as a youth to make the good confession could Jack remember feeling the Spirit as he did during the choir's performance that night. It was one solid hour of spiritually uplifting music. Songs that were not gospel songs were, nevertheless, just as uplifting. Jack heard Hannah sing for the first time. Her voice reminded him of Aretha Franklin. To close out the concert, the choir gave their rendition of the song Louie Armstrong made famous during the Vietnam War, "What a Wonderful World." The audience gave them a standing ovation.

Jack was glad to see a good number of black people in the audience, but as Zeb had predicted, he did not see anyone in the audience who did not attend church somewhere.

Melanie and Hannah informed him after the concert that this was their best concert to date and the love offering came to just over $1,500.

Jack knew bigger and better things were yet to come.

CHAPTER 32

GETTING READY FOR THE BIG EVENT

After hearing one of the best gospel concerts of his life, Jack was confident that if he put the right team together they could produce one of the most successful programs in the history of Cobbwebb County.

He wanted this event to be more than just a concert. He would promote it as *A Night to Remember*. He liked the idea of a dinner-concert and a program that the whole family could attend. And he knew just the place to have it: the AG Convention Center. He had attended a wedding reception there and knew it would easily seat more than 200 guests.

On Monday morning Jack met with the AG Center manager and made arrangements for the event on a Saturday night to be determined in late April when it was not booked.

Then Jack contacted those he wanted to serve on his team and invited them to his home the following night for dinner. The team consisted of J.R. Sampson; Ms. Sadie Tyson, choir director; and Pastor Isaias Washington and his daughters Melanie and Hannah.

They all arrived Tuesday shortly before six. Jack had worked hard to prepare a meal of grilled pork chops, sweet potatoes, black-eyed peas, carrots, applesauce, tossed salad, and chocolate pecan pie, much to his guests' appreciation

After dinner Jack briefed them on what Zeb Johnson had asked him to do. "I invited you here tonight because you are the ones who can make this project a success. All I can do is toss out some ideas and suggestions and bring all the parts together to make a whole.

"The Singing Disciples Choir is a hidden treasure in Cobbwebb County. The few concerts they have given in area churches have raised more than $2,500. The dinner-concert at the AG Center will draw people who believe but do not practice their faith through affiliation with a body of believers. If the concert is successful, and I have no doubt it will be, this could lead to even greater things for the choir. And more importantly, it could inspire people to look inward at their relationship with God."

All were elated to be asked to be a part of the team and agreed to do all they could to make this the best concert to date. Saturday night following the Easter school break was the date selected for the event. That would be the third Saturday night in April, and that date was open on the AG Center calendar.

"Ms. Sadie," Jack asked, "will a month be enough time for the choir to work up a completely new one-hour concert?"

"I think so. While I believe the choir will gladly accept this new challenge, I want them to make the decision. If we do the concert, what type of music do you want us to sing?"

"I'm thinking patriotic and inspirational songs, songs that would be popular with most any audience."

"I'll call you after choir practice Wednesday with an answer."

He asked J.R. to cater a buffet-style meal for 200-plus guests.

"I have served that many at the restaurant in one night but have not catered for a group this large," said J.R. "I want to discuss it with my employees before making a final decision."

"Thanks for your willingness to try something different, J.R., and I agree that those involved should be in on the decision making. Assuming we go forward with the concert, I suggest we have dinner from 6:30 to 7:30 p.m. The concert would start at 7:45." The team concurred with the schedule.

"How much will the tickets cost and who will be taking care of this part of the program?" asked Pastor Isaias.

"I recommend we go for 200 dinner tickets at twenty-five dollars each. Zeb Johnson will print the tickets and advertise the concert in *The Gazette*."

"I need someone to handle ticket sales," said Jack.

"I'll gladly take care of that," said Hannah.

"I don't think my regular pianist has the time to support the concert," said Ms. Sadie. "Do you know someone who would be willing to fill in for her if we decide to do this?"

Jack looked at Melanie and smiled. "I know you can do it," he said.

"If you believe I'm good enough, I'll do it."

"You're good enough," Hannah said.

"If there are no more questions or comments, we'll close the meeting," said Jack.

He thanked everyone for coming and called on Pastor Isaias to ask God to bless what they were attempting to do.

Pastor Isaias obliged.

By Friday he had received calls from J.R. and Ms. Sadie confirming that they would support the event. Jack asked Zeb to begin promoting ticket sales in Tuesday's paper. Jack would provide Zeb with the master copy of the tickets for printing Monday.

Jack was among the first to purchase tickets for himself and Mark and Sammie. It was a way to show his appreciation for what his brother had done with the memento project, which had raised more money than expected because many who purchased a memento paid more than the asking price.

Within a week of the article's appearance in *The Gazette*, most of the tickets had been sold. And they were all sold by the end of week two, except for the extras, which Jack was holding.

The choir collectively decided which songs to sing, picking those that best fit their voices and style from among oldies and modern tunes. Every song they chose was uplifting and patriotic or spiritual. They chose a dozen songs and Jack loved every one of them. He sat in on one of the practice sessions and was in awe of the talent coming from such a small group. He was certain that after this performance the choir would be in big demand.

A bevy of activity filled the lives of just about every member of The Ark of Salvation Church. Christ's Church was under construction and progressing as planned, the youth group was having yard sales every Saturday, the choir began practicing twice weekly, and the adult and youth Sunday school classes were working together to decorate the AG Center. One of their projects was the preparation of hand-painted signs depicting the different messages that would be presented through the music the choir would sing.

Meanwhile, Zeb Johnson had gotten the mayor to join him to welcome guests as they arrived. Zinnia volunteered to hand out programs to guests and to cover the event for the paper.

J.R. discussed the event with his employees and twelve waiters and waitresses volunteered to serve the food. All refused to accept pay and agreed to give all tips they received to the building fund. Because of that, J.R. was able to provide a gourmet meal for $10 each, which meant that the program would raise $3,000 on the sale of 200 tickets. The buffet table would offer fried and barbecued chicken, baked ham, roast beef, both sweet and Irish potatoes, a variety of vegetables, and fresh strawberry shortcake and pecan pie for desert.

Jack had headed up a multitude of events such as this during his Air Force career, but all of his backers were paid and expected to give 100 percent. He was amazed at the way the community had come together, young and old, black and white, to contribute to the rebuilding of Christ's Church. Not a single person from whom he'd requested help had turned him down. His job had been as easy as it was in the days when he had a general standing behind him. And when he really thought about it, he felt that he had someone more powerful than a general helping him now.

The day before the event, Jack called everyone to see if there were any last minute things that needed taking care of. All were excited and ready. That afternoon he worked with the Sunday school class members to decorate the AG Center, check the sound system, the AC, and general appearance of the facility. Everything was in order.

Silver and gold stars hung above the stage where the choir would perform, one star for each person in the choir. Hidden behind the choir was a circulating fan that when turned on would fan the stars, giving the impression they were dancing with the music.

The piano was on loan from The Clod Hoppers Music Center, and its owner, Mr. Archie Satterfield, had it delivered and tuned. Melanie had chosen this particular piano because it was one she was well acquainted with. The fee for this service was a note in the program thanking Mr. Satterfield for generously making it available for the concert.

Throughout the dining area were decorations and motivational signs: *What a Wonderful World, God Bless America, This is My Country, You'll Never Walk Alone, Everything is Beautiful, He's Got the Whole World in His Hands, God Bless the USA, Let Us Celebrate Life Together, We Are One in the Spirit, Oh Happy Day,* and many more.

The round tables were covered with red, white, and blue cloths. The napkins varied in colors and contained messages such as *Faith, hope, and love, Let us reason together, We are one in the Spirit, and God Bless the USA.* A single red rose adorned each table. *The Gazette*, sponsor of the dinner concert, spared no expense in converting the center into a place for refined dining and entertainment.

On his way home Jack stopped by the Dodge City Steak House to see J.R. He knew that both dinner and concert had to be good for the event to be successful. "I came by to see if you need any help getting everything in place for tomorrow night," Jack said.

"Thanks for the offer, but I've got more help than I need already. I can't believe how many people have offered to give me a hand. You'd think we were serving the president; everybody wants to be a part of it."

"This is more important than serving the president, J.R., and it's good to know that your friends and customers recognize that," Jack said with a big grin.

While visiting with J.R., Jack explained that he still had nine of the twenty-five spare tickets left. "If I sell those today or tomorrow will you have enough food to feed them?"

"Yes, we can handle that. In fact, there will be enough food to feed the choir after the concert."

"It's awful kind of you to do that, J.R. This wasn't a part of the deal, so what brought this on?"

"Well, everyone I know has done something to help build that church. I didn't want to be left out."

"I can't thank you enough," Jack said, and with that gave J.R. a big hug. Jack's admiration for his good friend had gone up yet another notch.

Friday night after Jack had eaten supper, he received a call from Will Webster.

"I hate to call you at the last minute, Jack, but both of my daughters and their husbands and my four grandchildren showed up unexpectedly today. While shopping this afternoon, the girls heard about the dinner-concert tomorrow night. And all of them want to go. Had I known they were going to be here, I would have called sooner. Can you help?"

"I'm glad you called, Will. I have exactly nine tickets remaining and I will be glad to drop them off at your home tomorrow. And since you were so generous in giving the land to the church, these are on me."

"That won't work for me, Jack. I appreciate your offer, but if I can't pay for the tickets, I'm not taking them. I gave the land to the church. I'm buying the tickets for me and my family. If I don't pay for the tickets, then I'm not giving my family anything. You are."

"I completely understand. I'd do the same thing if I were you, Will. My offer was just another attempt to let you know how much your gift to the church is appreciated."

"Thank you. You have made my day. I told my daughters all the tickets had been sold and they were so disappointed. That's why I called you, hoping that something could be done to get us in. How did you just happen to have nine tickets in your back pocket?"

"I had twenty-five extra tickets, Will. I learned long ago that it pays to put a few tickets in reserve for situations exactly like yours. There are no more tickets, so I'm praying that we do not have any more requests."

"My family will be overjoyed to hear the good news. Quite frankly, Jack, I am too. It's been a long time since the whole family has been together for an occasion such as this. Fact is, I can't remember if there was a last time."

"Wonderful! I'm looking forward to meeting and fellow-shipping with your family."

Jack knew Will was a good man who had become somewhat of a hermit after his wife died. He hoped the dinner-concert would serve to bring him into fellowship in the church. There he could find a new purpose in life and connect with others who could help to fill the void left by the passing of his spouse.

CHAPTER 33

THE THIRTEENTH SONG

Jack stayed in bed a little longer than usual Saturday morning because he knew it would be a long day. He needed the extra rest. And as he lay in bed all he could think about was the dinner-concert. *What have I missed? What could go wrong? Will all be well and will everyone be able to do their part?* Jack was working with some of Cobbwebb County's best people, and he told himself: *There is nothing to worry about.* He decided to get up and go forth, trusting and believing, and let go of any doubts that crept into his mind.

A soft rain was falling, but the weather forecast called for clear skies in the afternoon and temperatures in the midseventies. Even the weather was cooperating! It was going to be a great day, he decided!

After breakfast, Jack drove to Will's place to drop off the tickets and to meet his family. He spent an hour getting to know them. They were the kind of people he would love to have as neighbors. They were grateful for the tickets and were looking forward to the dinner-concert. So were their four children, two boys and two girls, all teenagers. Jack wanted to stay longer, but he didn't want to intrude on the family gathering. Before leaving, he invited them to church Sunday and urged them to bring Will with them.

After leaving the Webster family, Jack thought of something he had not done. The choir was meeting at the church around 6 p.m. and Jack wondered if they wanted something to eat before the concert, so he dropped by the pastor's home to inquire.

"We can't sing on a full stomach," said Hannah, "so we are going to have a small snack before we show up at the church for the final practice. We will be hungry after the concert. If you've got something for us then, we'll take it," she chided.

"It'll be waiting for you!" said Jack.

Hannah didn't believe him. "You're kidding, aren't you?"

"No. J.R. will have food for all of you when the concert ends and the crowd leaves the center."

"The rest of the choir will be happy to hear about that!"

Pastor Isaias was working on his sermon. As always, he was happy to see Jack. The two men sat in his study and chatted for a while, mostly about how the world had changed in so many ways and not very much in others.

The pastor asked Jack if he needed him to do anything other than the opening prayer.

"Not a thing. You will be seated at the table just in front of the stage along with your grandson Lamont, Zeb Johnson and his family, Zinnia Gregory, and me. Just enjoy the night."

"Our choir has never done anything like this and I'm a little anxious about the outcome," the pastor confided.

"There's nothing to worry about," Jack assured him. "The choir has put together a program of inspirational music that will warm even the coldest hearts. The choir is going to make its pastor a very proud man tonight."

Jack bid farewell to the pastor and Hannah and returned home.

He felt useless. There was nothing more he could do but wait until 6:30, and Jack detested waiting. So, to kill time, he decided to go to his favorite place: the forest at the north end of the farm. He walked the old cart path that divided the main ridge from the swamps on either side. The timber on the ridge was about ready for harvesting again, so the undergrowth was minimal. In most places, he could see all the way to the swamps on both sides of the ridge. The wind had picked up and a cold front was moving through. It was a good day to be in the woods.

Jack had always found the forest a place of refuge; tranquility and peace and quiet reigned there. There was some noise, but it was natural and belonged there. There was nothing to do when you walked in the forest but enjoy what you smelled, saw, and heard. You didn't have to rake the leaves or trim the bushes. Everything looked just fine the way it was.

The forest was the only place Jack could go and leave all his troubles and cares behind—there at the edge of the woods. When he entered the forest, an unexplainable change took place, something within like a chameleon that changes colors when it moves from one environment to another. As a boy he had walked this same path with a totally different view of the forest and the world he lived in. His life had come full circle. He had walked down many roads between the time he left the farm and when he returned just a few months earlier. This place in which he now found himself had always been a part of him. On too many occasions when trials and tribulations had invaded his life, Jack remembered this place of escape and wished he could come to it.

How fortunate he considered himself, not just to have a place like this to visit, but to have learned its true value in a world where so many have been attracted to the neon lights like insects.

Jack suddenly woke from his reverie and found himself standing on the south bank of Moccasin Ditch. He watched the water as it occasionally moved to indicate the presence of something within. He wondered if the herring still ran into the ditch in April and remembered how he used to catch them in a dip net at the mouth of the ditch.

As he stood there on the ditch bank, something unexpectedly crept into his mind that he could not suppress: Summer Brown. He knew she would love this place because he and Summer had often enjoyed time together walking in the parks around Gold City. As he thought of her, it occurred to him that no matter how big the net, he could never catch all the herring entering the ditch. The thought that Summer may have escaped suddenly blanketed him with sadness. It was time to go home and complete today's work.

By the time Jack walked back along the edge of the swamp to his pickup, it was well past 3 p.m. He returned home, took a shower, shaved, and dressed for the evening's gala. He left for the AG Center at 5:30.

Jack still felt useless. Everything was in place, and J.R. and his crew had set up two buffet lines, one on either side of the center. Shortly after 6 p.m. guests began arriving. The greeting crew was in place to meet them. Jack made it a point to shake hands with everyone and thank them for coming. When his brother Mark and wife Sammie arrived, he let them choose a place to sit, since they did not feel comfortable sitting near the stage.

By 6:30, ninety-five percent of all the seats were filled. Jack went to the microphone, welcomed everyone, and thanked all the people who were involved in making this event possible. He then invited Pastor Isaias to open the program with prayer.

The pastor's prayer was short and to the point, and guests were invited to help themselves in one of the two buffet lines.

Jack did not eat until all the guests had gone through the buffet line. He roamed the dining area to see if guests were enjoying their meal. He didn't have to ask. Plates were cleaned and many returned for more.

As the time approached for the choir to sing, people were beginning to wonder where the choir was because the stage was still empty.

Unbeknown to the audience, choir members had come in one at a time looking as if they were guests, but had slipped into a dressing room near the back of the AG Center to don their robes.

At the appointed time, Jack's responsibility was to get everyone's attention while the choir moved into position behind the audience.

Jack went to the microphone and asked if they had enjoyed their meal. That question received a big round of applause. Jack took the opportunity to thank J.R. Sampson and his staff for the excellent meal and service and explained that all the workers had given of their time freely for the benefit of rebuilding Christ's Church. That got another round of applause.

While Jack was speaking, the choir quietly exited the dressing room in their bright purple robes and surrounded the audience from every direction from the rear.

"I know you are wondering where the choir is," Jack continued, "and I am privileged to tell you that they are on their way to the stage."

And with that said, the soundman turned up the music to *This Is My Country* and choir members made their way through the audience to the stage singing the lyrics. When they finished the song on stage, the crowd gave them a standing ovation. For the next half hour every song the choir sang was a hit with the audience.

Although not on the agenda, Zeb Johnson interrupted the program at the midway point to make two announcements. The choir did not mind because it gave them a much-needed break.

After thanking everyone for supporting the dinner-concert, Zeb said, "I am proud to announce that your newspaper, *The Gazette,* has been selected as the top biweekly newspaper in the state by the Carolina Press Association for its outstanding promotion of events and activities which bring the community together."

This drew a big round of applause. Zeb then asked Zinnia to join him on the stage. "I think just about everyone in the county knows Zinnia Gregory.

"I also learned yesterday that Zinnia's superb reporting has won her the association's top reporter award."

That drew an even bigger round of applause.

"Now, I have some bad news for us, but good news for Zinnia. Since day one her goal has been to return to the District of Columbia and work for one of the big-name dailies. Yesterday she accepted an offer from the *Post* and will be leaving in two weeks for Washington."

The audience gave her a standing ovation. For the first time since her almost three-year stay in Cobbwebb County, Zinnia realized how much she was appreciated, not only by her boss and coworkers, but by the people who had come to know her through the stories she had written for the paper. She could not hold back the tears as she bowed and waved to the audience, thanking them for their expression of kindness and adoration.

The second half of the concert was just as successful as the first. The choir chose to sing "What a Wonderful World" to close out the program.

After the applause finally subsided, Melanie announced that she and Hannah had one more surprise for the audience, a thirteenth song, not included in the program. Even Jack was unaware of this addition to the program. While other choir members exited the stage, Melanie spoke to the audience:

"Hannah, my sister, and I want to tell you why this world has been so wonderful to us. We were blessed with two wonderful parents. Our mother has passed on, but our dad is still with us. We are dedicating this final song tonight to him. Dad was our Moses when we got lost in the wilderness; he was our Joshua when we needed to cross another river, and when we came to the forks in the roads of our lives, he was our Apostle Paul, always encouraging us to take the high road. I know everyone will recognize this song, and I hope it will inspire you to honor those who have made yours a wonderful world, too."

The music began, and Melanie and Hannah sang the classic, "Wind beneath My Wings." Pastor Isaias sat motionless as his daughters poured their hearts and souls into the song. He was not accustomed to such public recognition. He could not hold back the tears.

The response from the audience was overwhelming: five minutes of continuous applause.

The old pastor joined his daughters on stage in a warm embrace and they cried together. It was the most emotional moment Jack had ever witnessed. He noticed that Will's daughters were hugging him, no doubt an after effect of the final song. Families Jack did not know were doing the same.

Jack had planned to close out the night's program with a few comments but decided against it. He had wanted to say *Blessed is the man who has two daughters like Melanie and Hannah,* but felt it was not needed. So he simply let the audience fade away with the image they saw of the pastor and his two daughters embracing on the stage. He could not think of any words that would outdo that image.

Even without the surprises, the dinner-concert had fulfilled its objective as a night to remember. Jack felt a sense of relief. As good as the program looked on paper, it turned out to be far better than he had imagined.

Once again, he had received much more than he felt he deserved and was grateful to the One who had worked all things for good to those involved in the night's program.

CHAPTER 34

THE NEW CHRIST'S CHURCH

Jack was up early Sunday morning, and instead of having breakfast at home as he normally did, he decided to support one of the local restaurants. He chose the Barnyard Café, a popular restaurant with most residents, and a place where one could catch up on what was happening in the community.

It was busy as usual, and because all the booths were occupied, Jack took a seat at the counter. After the waitress took his order, he casually looked around the restaurant and began listening to what people were talking about. Among the hot topics that morning was the dinner-concert the night before at the AG Center. Some had been present and others were just relating what they had heard from those in attendance. A few who entered the restaurant recognized Jack and came by to tell him how much they enjoyed the choir and the idea of the dinner-concert. Some wanted to know when they could expect to attend another like it. He was not surprised by what he heard.

When he arrived for the early worship service, the parking lot was almost full. Inside the sanctuary, he had to take a seat up front and the ushers were adding extra chairs that were also filled before the service began. Will and his entire family were there. He saw several others who were at the concert the night before. Jack knew he was seeing the after-effects of the previous night's event in the church, fulfilling the second and most important objective of the big event.

This was the first time the early service had been packed to overflowing since Pastor Isaias had started two services in January. The pastor was amazed to see a full house and so many new faces, both black and white.

The subject of his sermon that morning was taken from the experience of the Prophet Elijah, who fled King Ahab and Queen Jezebel for fear of his life and hid in a cave on Mt. Horeb. In a still small voice, God asked Elijah what he was doing in the cave.

Pastor Isaias built his sermon around this question. It was a powerful message that called people from their caves, where they could do nothing, and encouraged them to get back into the arena where they could serve mankind.

"The greatest story ever told had to be lived before it could be told," he said. "I challenge you to ask yourself this question: 'What am I doing here?' If all you are doing is sitting on the sidelines, you are not where God wants you to be, and you're not doing what God needs you to do."

As Jack watched dozens respond to the altar call, he was convinced that the choir's performance at the AG Center had started something big in Cobbwebb County. He prayed that it would spread throughout the land and that it would live a long life.

In Tuesday's *Gazette*, Zeb Johnson fueled the flames with two full pages of photos and stories about the dinner-concert. Everyone who had a hand in making it such a success was recognized. Zinnia's stories focused on the program from the perspective of the attendees, and everyone she interviewed said it was indeed a night to remember.

For the next two weeks, the talk of the county was the dinner-concert. The choir received so many requests to perform that many of them were turned down for lack of time. The choir continued to perform one concert each week for a love offering and became the church's number one fundraiser.

Jack had hired the Winston Arts Club to record the show and produce 100 compact discs, which were made available for purchase for those who could not attend the dinner-concert. He paid for their services and gave the CDs to Zeb Johnson, who advertised their availability and sold them for $10 each and gave the money to Christ's Church building fund.

Well before the church building was completed, enough funds had been raised to rebuild Christ's Church without having to borrow a dime. Still needed, however, was money to purchase pews, a podium, a piano, tables and chairs for classrooms and the fellowship hall, a cook stove, a fridge, items for the nursery, a sound-video system, and a host of other items. Another $30,000 was needed. And it too was raised before the opening service. Funds came in from increased attendance, additional publicity generated through the choir, from the choir's performances, and the yard sales the youth were holding each Saturday. People who had heard about the resurrection of the church and all the efforts being undertaken to rebuild it sent money. The pastor also received a check for the old coins for $5,500.

An open house was held the last Saturday in June, the day before the first service. Hundreds of people from the county and other parts of the state came to tour the new facility. J.R. Sampson and several other vendors were present to provide food and beverages.

Pastor Isaias was overjoyed when he saw the church Norm Miller and his company had built. When he was presented with the keys, he wept. "These are tears of pure joy," he said. "When I think of where we came from and see this fine facility, how can I keep from shedding tears of joy. Not too long ago I was beginning to think this would not happen in my lifetime. This is an answer to prayers from many people, and the fulfillment of a dream that I could not turn loose. Praise God!" he cried.

Jack saw two things about the new church that were different. The community—including Christians, non-Christians, blacks, whites, and locals, as well as people from many others states—supported the resurrection of the church by putting money in the pot to see the facility built. Not a dime was borrowed to build the church.

Also different was the way boards from the old church were used to enhance the beauty of the new, and thus connecting the past with the present. *People who do not know the history of the church will not see this connection,* Jack thought. *But that's true of people, too. We are all connected to the past as surely as we are a link to the future.*

In many ways the church was like others of its day. The baptistery was directly behind the choir section, which was on a two-foot high platform that also included the pulpit in the center and to one side, the piano. Below the pulpit was the altar.

Boards from the old church had been smoothed and varnished and used as part of the raised platform that was visible to the congregation. Pews from the old church building had been refurbished and resized for members to kneel on when they came to the altar. The communion table was a gift from Norm Miller. It too was made from the boards he had purchased from the old church building. He had incorporated the past into the present in such a way that only those who knew the history of the church would understand the significance of what they were seeing when they looked at the pulpit and altar area. It was magnificent.

Jack's brother Mark made one other contribution to the new building. He took the boards from the old cabinet that once contained the title to the church, the logbook, and quill, and built a new cabinet with glass doors. The three items were displayed in the cabinet, which was mounted on the wall in the foyer. One final touch of class from Norm Miller and his construction workers: the signs identifying each of the different rooms in the facility were made from the old church boards: Nursery, Adult Class, Youth, etc. In the fellowship hall was a painting of the old Christ's Church building sitting at the fork in the road. This gift came from Jack's good friend Ron Cratt in Salem, and the painting was framed with boards from the old church.

Viewed from the north bend in the Poopah River, the beauty and grandeur of Christ's Church was breathtaking. Jack had no doubt that it would be the subject of many postcards.

The steeple was situated directly over the choir, pulpit, and alter. It rose forty feet into the Carolina blue sky. Atop the white steeple was a white cross that glittered in the sunlight. It could be seen from anywhere in Winston. Christ's Church had literally become the new light on a hill in Winston, the culmination of a dream that went far beyond the expectations of the dreamers.

Three shades of light brown bricks were laid in an alternating pattern that accentuated the tan shingle roof. Tan vinyl covered the eaves, protecting the wood from carpenter bees. Two concrete handicap ramps with black iron railings, one on each side of the portico entryway, made it easy for elderly and handicapped worshipers to enter the sanctuary. Brick steps, also with iron railings, graced the front of the portico.

The beauty in the simplicity of the church was apparent from any angle. Christ's Church was a shining testimony to the commitment, faith, hard work, and community spirit of all who stood behind Pastor Isaias and his dream.

While helping to make the pastor's dream a reality, the community discovered the joy that comes from giving. And those who contributed to the fruition of the pastor's dream could look at Christ's Church and say, *Look what God has done through us.*

CHAPTER 35

A NEW BEGINNING

Anticipating a huge crowd for the first Sunday service, Pastor Isaias decided to conduct two morning services, one at 8:30 and the second at 10:30. A new pastor had arrived and was in place to conduct services at The Ark of Salvation Church, freeing Pastor Isaias to devote all of his energies to put the resurrected Christ's Church on a solid foundation.

"So many people have been involved in getting this church rebuilt," the pastor said, "and I do not want to turn anyone away. I know many who have contributed will come to see what we have done and are doing. I would like to think we would need two services every week, but it will take some time before that happens."

The pastor's thinking was on target. While neither service filled every seat in the new sanctuary, it was very close in both services. One service alone would never have accommodated all the people who turned out that first Sunday.

Participating in both services was the choir from The Ark of Salvation Church. The choir sang one of their favorites, "Go Tell It on the Mountain," and just before the pastor's message Melanie sang "I Believe in Miracles" by John W. Peterson. While the music was sufficient to make the first Sunday's worship service a success, Pastor Isaias added some frosting.

His topic for the day was miracles. "I know there are people who don't believe in miracles, but not believing does not stop

217

miracles from happening. Miracles happen all the time. We just fail to see them as such. It's not until something really big happens, something way above the norm, that we even think about it.

"The resurrection of this church is a miracle. I have never seen anything like this in my fifty-plus years of ministry. I have not even heard of anything like this happening. If I could explain to you in some logical way what has happened, I would not call this a miracle. But I can't explain it, because miracles cannot be explained.

"You can tell a miracle is in progress when things begin to happen for no reason at all. Eight months ago Elder Jeremiah and I were standing in front of the old dilapidated church building wondering what to do with it. We thought it was worthless and were thinking of asking the fire department to burn it down.

"But along came this white man who had just moved back to the county. It just so happened that he saw us standing in front of the church, and for some reason even he could not explain, he stopped to ask some questions about the building. That's when things began to happen beyond the ordinary. Instead of destroying the building, it was turned into a gold mine. Through his efforts we discovered that the first church had been built not by blacks, but by blacks and whites in the community.

"In the process of selling the boards from the church building, it just so happened that we discovered the man who built the facility we are worshipping in this morning. He purchased most of the boards from the old church and used some of them for our altar and in other places in the building.

"As word spread about the resurrection of the church, people began to respond from throughout the country. While funds poured in to rebuild Christ's Church, we were having difficulty finding land on which to build. Then it just so happened that another white man came forward and for one dollar an acre sold us the property on which this church is sitting.

"I'm telling you, brothers and sisters, that all these things did not happen on their own. The Master had a plan that we could not see unfolding, but as we look back on the events of the past eight months, we can clearly see that God had a hand in everything. He has worked all things to our good.

"This church is not the only thing that has been revived. The relationship between blacks and whites in this community has been taken to a new level. I see more white people in this audience this morning than I saw in my first fifty years of ministry. We are traveling down a new road together, and I believe things will only get better for us and for our community.

"And I have seen a revival in the lives of many people. The work of our choir has been a great inspiration to me and to the community, and it has brought us closer together. Their beautiful voices have carried the gospel message to places I could not have gone, and in doing so, they have earned a name for themselves and brought great distinction to our congregation.

"My daughter Melanie quit singing and playing the piano when her mother died. She is now our pianist. I don't think this would have happened had it not been for the great work which has been in progress for the past eight months.

"That white man whom we met for the first time in front of the old church building confessed to me that he too has been revived.

"When we let God change us, it is always for our good. And I know a lot of people have been changed for good."

In closing his message, the pastor became more somber.

"Finally, I have to confess that I too was resurrected from my slumber. I promised my mother before she died that I would rebuild that old church in Winston. At the age of seventy-five, and not one penny in the bank for the project, I was about ready to give up my dream. Then along came this white man. All this stranger had to offer us were some ideas and a willingness to do something he had never done before, and that was to reach out to this old preacher and offer to help me fulfill my dream."

Pastor Isaias could not hold back the tears and neither could many in the audience

"God is good," Pastor Isaias said.

"All the time," the congregation responded.

As the choir sang "Just as I Am," the pastor encouraged his audience to experience the goodness of God. "If you are standing at the fork in the road this morning, or if you have been hiding in a cave, I urge you take the high road and walk with the living Christ. We still have much work to do, and God is inviting you to be a laborer in His vineyard. Come just as you are," he pleaded, "and let God make you the person you ought to be."

Many came forward that morning, including the white man who revived the preacher's dream. He was among the first to place his membership with the resurrected Christ's Church.

When things went well, Jack's old Air Force boss would say that all the planets were lined up just right. That's exactly how Jack felt about what had happened for Pastor Isaias and his dream. As for himself, there was still one planet missing.

CHAPTER 36

A LETTER FROM ZINNIA

That summer passed quickly. The newly resurrected church became a vibrant part of the community and added new members almost weekly. Melanie and Hannah rounded up enough voices to start a choir. A new minister was hired to take over when Pastor Isaias retired at the beginning of the following year. Jack agreed to teach the adult Bible class, giving the pastor more time to perform pastoral duties. The church was alive and well, there was a sense of togetherness, agape love abounded, and Jack believed the Spirit was present in everything the church did. He also believed he was exactly where he was supposed to be and doing exactly what God wanted him to do.

One morning in early September he came home from cutting firewood and found a letter from Zinnia in his mailbox. It was the first time he had heard from her since she mailed him a post card in May announcing her new address. He had sent her a card congratulating her once again on making it into the big-time world of journalism.

After making a sandwich for lunch, he sat down to eat and enjoy the lone piece of good mail he had received in quite some time. "Dear Jack," it began,

> *Please forgive me for not writing sooner. Just getting to know my way around D.C. has been a part-time job*

221

and learning the ropes of reporting at this level has been quite a challenge.

I guess I am doing OK because yesterday when I said farewell to my boss for the day he made the comment "Jack was right about you." So I asked him, "Who are you talking about?" and he told me "Jack Porter." And that was when I found out that you had sent Jason Widener some of the articles I had written and told him that if he was looking for an outstanding reporter to contact Zinnia Gregory. Then he told me about the times you and he were stationed together on Guam during the Vietnam War.

Not until then did I realize that you are the one responsible for me getting this job. I wondered why Jason had called and offered me the job in the first place. I was so excited at the time about getting the job I had dreamed of that I never thought about it.

Now that I know that it was all your doing, this is to officially thank you from the bottom of my heart. And while I am in the thanksgiving mood, thank you for the delicious box of chocolates you gave me. I know who the Secret Admirer is now, too.

In the apartment complex where I lived in Winston there was an old woman named Inez who lived with her daughter and her husband. I can't remember her last name, but I remember her telling everyone about this white man who fixed her car. She said she told him that she could not pay for it and that the man fixed it anyway. She said the man told her that God sent him there to fix the car and gave him the money to pay for it. Nobody paid much attention to her story at the time.

If my memory serves me right, that happened about the same time Jack Porter returned to Cobbwebb County. And it sounds like something you would say and do. I believe God sent you there for reasons other than fixing Inez's car.

As you know, when I took the job at The Gazette I signed on because it was the only job available to this new college grad. The pay was not that good, the location for a young single woman was awful, and I felt alone and isolated from the rest of the world. My one and only goal was to get out of there as fast as I could.

Now more than three years later I look back on my experience and the people I met and tell myself that I would not have wanted it any other way. I was revived along with that church, that community, and probably a bunch of other people.

I learned, Jack, that a place is not defined by its location but by its people. I will be looking for people in D.C. like Zeb Johnson, Pastor Isaias and his daughters Hannah and Melanie, and yes, you too, Jack. When I think of Winston in the future, it will bring back the memories of these people and the many others I came to know, love, and admire for their honesty, kindness, and commitment to changing our world for the better.

My next goal in life is to find a man like Jack Porter that I can share my life with. Please pray for that to happen.

Thanks again for everything. If you ever stray this far north, I would love to see you again. Dinner is on me.

Your Grateful Friend in D.C.,
Signed Zinnia Gregory

Jack smiled as he remembered the beautiful young black girl he had had the privilege of knowing for a few short months. He knew it was not he who had gotten her the job; it was her talent. All he did was make it known to an old Air Force buddy who he knew would recognize it as well, and give her a chance to excel. And he had no doubt that she would excel, and in a city the size of Washington, God would help her find a suitable soul mate.

CHAPTER 37

TOGETHER AGAIN

Of all the days and events in the life of Jack Porter since his return to the place in which he was raised, none would be remembered better than what happened on Saturday, September 17, the year in which he celebrated his sixtieth birthday.

He had become accustomed to sleeping in on Saturday mornings, having a late breakfast, and once his body was fully awake, he would enjoy the day visiting friends and relatives. He also enjoyed walking the path along the Poopah River with Hannah, weather permitting.

While enjoying his breakfast in the sunroom where he could see the morning unfold in his backyard, Jack's mind drifted back to his early youth as he watched two squirrels gathering nuts. What stood out to him about his youth on this particular morning was his lack of material possessions. About all he had then were the essentials of life: plenty of good food, a roof over his head, hand-me-down clothes, and parents that loved him. And yet, as he remembered those days, he could not think of anything that he was missing in his life even though he did not have any of the things that the *well-to-do* possessed. He was simply content with what he had.

Sitting in the same home five decades later Jack realized he had far more in material things than he had ever dreamed of. He remembered reading about one of America's richest men who was on his deathbed. Someone asked him if there was anything else he wanted before he died. His answer was *one more dollar.*

While thinking about this man's love for money, Jack was also listening to WINS Radio. On Saturday mornings the DJ played golden oldies, and the one they began the show with this morning opened the curtain of his memory back to 1959. It was the year he met and married his wife, Misty. Jack would never forget the theme song to the movie *A Summer Place.* He could not remember anything about the film, but its theme song was unforgettable. He wanted to dance with his wife again every time he heard it. All he and his wife had when that song was the most popular tune in America was each other, and their hopes and dreams of their life together. *When you are in love what else do you need?* he thought. He would gladly give up all of his possessions if he could and go back to that place and start life all over again with Misty.

Jack's state of reverie was interrupted when the doorbell rang. He thought he was hearing things at first, because his doorbell rarely rang on Saturday mornings. When it did, he usually hollered to whomever it was to come in, but he had not unlocked the door on this morning.

Jack arrived at the door on the second ring, expecting to see Mark or some other relative. But when he opened the door, he was shocked and could hardly believe his eyes. It was Summer Brown. After nearly a year, Jack had almost given up on ever seeing her again. Now, she was standing at his front door, and the man who could always find something to say was speechless.

Summer looked pale and there was much anxiety in her hazel eyes, but she was still beautiful to Jack. She had lost weight that she did not need to lose. She was wearing orange pants and a white blouse that seemed to highlight her pale face and empty eyes. With half a smile, she looked at Jack and asked, "Am I among the memories of the old man who lives here?"

With tears in his eyes, Jack stepped out onto the porch, put his arms around her, and said, "You bet you are, and you have been since the day I moved in. I still love you as much as ever, Summer Brown."

She began to sob uncontrollably. Jack could sense that his words had relieved her of a great burden, that he had without knowing it said exactly what Summer wanted to hear. They stood on the porch embracing each other until she stopped crying.

Jack could not find the words to express the joy that filled his heart at seeing Summer again. He hoped she could see this on his face. He invited her into his home and made a fresh pot of coffee, something he knew she would want. He offered to fix her breakfast.

"I can't eat now, Jack, but thank you for your kind offer and for making coffee for me."

All Jack could do was look at Summer, and there was so much he wanted to say to her, but he did not know where to begin.

He finally came up with, "I've missed you, Summer. How have you been?" That produced another outburst of tears.

Jack reached out to her and held her hands. "You don't have to tell me anything, Summer. Let the past lie in its dormant state."

When Summer stopped crying, she looked at Jack and said, "The past year has been the worst of my life. I must tell you about it, and I don't want you to feel sorry for me because I brought it all on myself."

Before she began, Jack poured two cups of coffee and they moved from the living room to the dinette area where they could view the small grove of cypress trees in the swampy area near the house. They sat at the small dining table facing each other. Jack could not remove his gaze from her.

"There's so much I want to tell you, Jack, that I hardly know where to begin. My world collapsed the night you told me you were returning to Winston. I convinced myself that you had walked out on me. That was not true, but I believed it at the time.

"Instead of taking responsibility for my actions, I blamed everything on you. I talked myself into hating you. I did not return your phone calls, answer the door when you came, or even read the cards and letters you sent. I threw the mail in a box. I don't know why I didn't toss them in the trash.

"I quit going to church. When my friends saw me they would ask where you were, which would upset me all the more. I became a hermit, an invisible member of the community.

"Not too long ago I returned to Pennsylvania to visit family and friends. While there I went shopping in one of the retail stores. At the checkout counter, the cashier asked, 'Do you remember me?' I looked her over and had to admit that if I ever knew her I did not remember. Then she told me she was Donna Simpson. I was shocked. She looked nothing like the pretty and charming high school senior who could pick and choose anyone she wanted to date. She was the happiest girl in the class and all the other girls envied her. I asked if we could get together after she got off work, and she invited me to her apartment.

"I learned that the girl I thought had it all had nothing. She told me she'd had two failed marriages, both to abusive men. She was living in a one-bedroom apartment in one of the poorest sections of town. She made little more than minimum wage. She had given up on men and found very little joy in life.

"She said her life changed when the boy she had made a commitment to caught her dating another classmate. That boy is now the town mayor and a successful businessman. 'I was a fool,' she said. 'I had everything a girl could hope for, but didn't know it at the time. I kept reaching out for more and wound up with nothing. It is sad to have what you really want in life and not know it until after you have lost it,' she told me.

"'I have thought of you often Summer. You don't know how much I admired you after I realized what I had done to myself. You were the one who had it all.'

"Her story shocked me, Jack. When I told you I was living the dream of my life, I was modeling my life after hers. Truth is, I was living in Fantasyland.

"I quit hating you and started hating myself.

"I thought about calling you after I returned home, but I couldn't believe you would want to hear from me after the way I had treated you.

"I decided to open the mail you sent me. In every piece of correspondence you told me that you loved me. I knew you were not lying to me, but I asked myself *How could anyone love someone as selfish, self-centered, and as ungrateful as I was?*

"I remembered all the things you did for me during the nine months we dated. You bowed down to my every whim, took me wherever I wanted to go, cared for my yard, home, and vehicle. I didn't thank you for anything or send you a card expressing my appreciation for the hundreds of acts of kindness you showed me or for any of the flowers and gifts you gave me.

"I found the courage to return to church and answered the first altar call. I asked God to forgive me for what I had done to you. I know God has forgiven me, but I'm finding it difficult to forgive myself. Pastor Gregory told me you had come by to see me. I was not home for that visit."

Summer became silent, looking out the window, thinking perhaps of what she wanted to say next.

Jack took her cup, rinsed it, and refilled it with coffee.

"Thanks, Jack. I came to see you for many reasons. I had to tell you what my life has been like since we last saw each other. While I could have been with you all this time, I was alone, lost in a world of make believe, bitterness, shame, and remorse.

"We were both blind. Your love for me was so great that you could not see my many imperfections. And I was so wrapped up in myself that I could not see the awesome man that so desperately wanted to share the rest of his life with me. I loved you, but I loved myself more.

"I am ashamed to think that I had the gall to ask you to stand by and watch me act like some homecoming queen and make a fool of myself before deciding what I wanted to do with the rest of my life.

"I came to thank you with all my heart for being so good to me, for being so patient with me, and for showing me more kindness than I deserved. I beg your forgiveness."

With his eyes still glued to Summer, Jack listened as the woman he loved more than anything else poured out her heart and soul. He wanted to cry and shout for joy at the same time.

"I forgave you a long time ago, Summer."

"There's another reason I came to see you, Jack. I want to start over. I can't live alone with the memories I have.

"If you have not found someone else, and if you still want me, I want you to take me to dinner, and after we eat, I want you to ask me the question that I could not answer the last time we dined together."

For the first time in his life, joy overflowed Jack's soul through uncontrollable tears. He stood and took Summer in his arms. They held each other until they stopped crying.

"There has not been another woman in my life since I met you," Jack said to Summer. "And there will never be another. What has happened has made us better human beings and in our suffering God has done a wonderful work in us.

"Today you have made me the happiest man in the world because I know the answer to the question I am going to ask you tonight. I've longed for this day, Summer, since the night I left you in tears."

With that, the two hugged and kissed, again and again and again. It was a long time before they let go of each other.

THE END

EPILOGUE

Jack proposed to Summer that night over dinner at the Dodge City Steak House. One week after their engagement, Pastor Isaias married Jack Porter and Summer Brown, the first white couple to exchange wedding vows in Christ's Church. And it was the first white couple that Pastor Isaias had married. Jack and Summer had not planned to make a big fuss over their wedding. But Jack's brother Mark and his wife Sammie, J.R. Sampson, and other friends in community came up with another plan.

When Jack and Summer arrived at the church shortly before 6 p.m. the parking lot was full. One slot had been reserved at the front entrance for *The Bride and Groom*. For the first time the new church was filled to overflowing. A reception was held in the fellowship hall after the wedding ceremony. J.R. Sampson called it a love feast "because it was done out of love for Jack and his new bride."

Following the Sunday morning service in which Jack and Summer were again recognized, the couple left Winston for their honeymoon in New England. Both wanted to see the fall colors and it would give Jack the opportunity to introduce his new bride to the members of Misty's family who still lived in that part of the country.

Christ's Church became a shining beacon in the Winston community. It was no longer a black church or white church, but a church where all of God's children worshipped together in harmony and brotherly love.

Jack knew he was a child of a loving God who worked all things for the good of those who love Him. If he ever had any doubts about that they were erased that Saturday in September when Summer Brown came back into his life for good. She was the planet that had been missing.

ABOUT THE AUTHOR

Jasper (Jay) E. Barber is the twenty-first of twenty-two offspring born to the late William Frank Barber and the fifth of six children born to the late Icelene Davenport Barber. He was born November 9, 1938, in Martin County, North Carolina.

He attended school in Jamesville, North Carolina, from 1945 to 1956. In November of 1956 he quit school in the eleventh grade and he enlisted in the United States Air Force the following month.

He remained in the Air Force until October 1, 1980, retiring with twenty-four years of service as a senior master sergeant. During that time he worked in public relations, recruiting, and acquired his writing skills while serving as a reporter, editor, and historian.

He attended Martin Community College in Williamston, North Carolina, from 1981 to 1982 and East Carolina University in nearby Greenville from 1982 to 1984. He graduated Magna Cum Laude with a Bachelor of Science Degree in English, the only child of Frank or Icelene Barber to graduate from college.

In August 1984 he accepted a job with the public affairs office at Seymour Johnson Air Force Base in Goldsboro, North Carolina. He became the deputy chief of public affairs for the world-renowned Fourth Fighter Wing and served in that position until retiring a second time on March 1, 2001.

This is his first novel. His first book, *Memories of the Islands: The Life, Place, and Times of the Barber Family*, was published in 2007.

He married Mary Jane Rogers in Brewer, Maine, on October 2, 1959. They have two sons: Dean and wife Sheila; Larry and wife Mary Ida; a granddaughter, Kelly; grandson, Chad; and great grandson Kayne Edwards.

He enjoys gardening, golfing, hiking, fishing, photography, spending time with family and friends, and studying the Bible. One of his favorite verses of scripture is Romans 8:28.

Jay and Mary reside in Goldsboro.